"You mig...
you slee...

Casey's voice was filled with outrage as she turned slowly to face John. He was still nestled comfortably under her covers—as if they'd actually slept together.

John made no effort to rise. "I did make a grab for my trousers before you dragged me in here. You were so eager to get me into your bed . . ."

"Very funny. I just assumed you were wearing something."

"I always sleep in the raw, but even if I didn't, all my clothes are next door."

Casey shook her head in wonder. "This has been the craziest day. Please go to bed."

"I am in bed."

"Don't do this to me. I've already made enough mistakes for one day. If Santa's out there making a list of who's been naughty . . ."

John drew Casey toward him. His lips touched hers in a breath of a kiss. "Then I'd say we're about to top the list. . . ."

Elise Title 's latest Temptation captures the zany humor and glorious romance of the Hollywood comedies of the 1930s. This is a romp in the best screwball tradition. Yet Elise has crafted such warm, believable characters that readers are bound to laugh *and* cry.

Elise has thirty novels to her credit under the name Alison Tyler, and *Too Many Husbands* is her fourth Temptation. The Title family lives in Hanover, New Hampshire.

Books by Elise Title

HARLEQUIN TEMPTATION
203—LOVE LETTERS
223—BABY, IT'S YOU!
266—MACNAMARA AND HALL

HARLEQUIN INTRIGUE
97—CIRCLE OF DECEPTION
119—ALL THROUGH THE NIGHT

Too Many Husbands

ELISE TITLE

Harlequin Books

TORONTO • NEW YORK • LONDON
AMSTERDAM • PARIS • SYDNEY • HAMBURG
STOCKHOLM • ATHENS • TOKYO • MILAN

To Jeff . . .
the only husband for me

Published January 1990

ISBN 0-373-25382-6

Prologue

Jingle bells, jingle bells . . .

"GET ME A HUSBAND!"

The two clerks could hear the sharp command through the closed door of Casey Croyden's office.

Marsha Williams stopped filing. "Did I hear right?" she asked, turning to Sue Mintnor at the next desk.

"What does she want with another husband?" Sue wondered aloud. "She dumped the first one after less than six months."

"No, she didn't dump him. He dumped her."

George, the mail clerk delivering parcels to the next cubicle, popped his head around the partition. "He didn't dump her. He was nuts about her. Let's face it. Croyden's some dish even if she is top brass. The way I heard it Croyden was married to her job and refused to take off with hubby when he had overseas travel assignments."

Grace Squier, standing at the nearby watercooler, shook her head. "Baloney," she said, coming over to join the group. "Wes Carpenter was a regular Casanova. I heard that Croyden found him and one of his lady friends—"

"Oh, no," Alice Burton, a typist from the next cubicle, popped around the partition and broke in. "If anything it was the other way around."

"Casey Croyden fooled around on the sly?" Marsha wrinkled her brow. "She was too busy rising up the corporate ladder to fool around on her husband, never mind have an affair. She's just turned twenty-eight and she's already head of acquisitions. Anyway, Croyden isn't the cheating type. She's tough, but she's a straight arrow."

Sue Mintnor agreed. "She may be hell on wheels to work for, but she doesn't ask any more of us than she asks of herself."

Alice Burton grinned broadly. "Oh, yeah? What about this bit about ordering a new husband?"

Just as Alice finished her remark the door to Casey Croyden's office opened. Alan Fisher, assistant director of acquisitions at Hammond Hotel Inc., and Les Rosen, Croyden's research coordinator, stepped out, giving each other rueful looks.

"What do you think? Can she pull it off?" the balding, haggard-looking Rosen asked, stopping at the watercooler to pour himself a drink.

Fisher, a tall, lanky fellow in his early thirties, shrugged, wiping his brow with the handkerchief he'd been palming all during the morning meeting. "Name me one thing she hasn't pulled off, I may have my hassles with Croyden at times, but there's no denying she's brilliant, daring and just about the most fiercely determined negotiator I've ever come across."

Rosen rubbed his jaw, "I know, I know. But this is different. Matoki isn't some Oriental rube, you know. The guy didn't become president of Japan's number one luxury hotel chain by chance. The research we dug up on Matoki makes him out to be one hell of a hard-nosed businessman even if he is very traditional and wedded to the old Japanese ways outside of work."

"Yeah, but the way Casey's playing it is brilliant." Fisher swallowed the cup of water.

The two men started off down the hall, Rosen's last remark filtering back to the crew around Sue Mintnor's desk. "I'd feel a lot better if she didn't have to play it with a phony husband."

As soon as Rosen and Fisher were out of hearing distance, George, the mail clerk, nodded sagely. "Okay, okay, ladies, the pieces are beginning to fall into place."

The four women eyed him expectantly.

"You know about Matoki, don't you?" George gave them a smug look, knowing full well they didn't.

"We know," Alice said, not to admit total defeat, "that he's head of Japan's biggest luxury hotel chain."

"Yeah," George drawled, "but do you know that our Casey, as well as every acquisition head of every hotel chain in the good old U.S. of A., has been trying to work a deal with Matoki for over a year now?"

"How do you know that?" Marsha gave him a doubting look.

"I got eyes. I got ears."

"Yeah," Grace said, "and you have access to all the mail coming through to Croyden's office. Didn't your mother ever teach you it wasn't right to read other people's private correspondence?"

George looked duly affronted. "I never read anything marked private. I just got a knack for picking up things. And I've got a good buddy working for the Archway Hotel group and another over at Graham. They pick up things, too. Everyone's hot to trot with Matoki. And it looks like our Casey is about to beat out the competition."

"Beat them out of what?" Grace asked.

"A real sweetheart of a deal. I wouldn't be surprised if this deal moves Croyden up a few notches. Maybe even a vice presidency."

"So what kind of a deal already?" Marsha asked impatiently.

"Matoki's thinking of doing some American-style hotels in Japan, and the way I hear it, he might take on an American partner."

Sue Mintnor frowned. "I still don't get it. What's that got to do with a husband?"

George hadn't the slightest idea, but he was saved from having to admit it because Croyden's door swung open again. This time it was Jane West who exited. Jane, a petite, perky redhead, was Casey Croyden's trusty, efficient executive assistant. She scrutinized the group gathered around the desk and gave them a rueful smile.

"You heard?"

"We heard her ordering up a husband," Marsha said.

"Yeah, kind of the same way she orders a hot pastrami for lunch," Sue observed.

Jane grinned. "Hot pastrami, a husband... hey, what's the difference? One you phone down to the deli for, the other you . . ."

"Phone your local matchmaker?" Grace offered.

"She only wants a husband for a couple of weeks," Jane said. "And she wants him by Saturday. Know any great husband types looking for a part-time gig?"

Marsha snorted. "I don't think there are any great husband types."

"Did you say by Saturday? Today's Thursday," George pointed out.

Jane gave him a narrow look. "Tell me about it."

Alice sighed. "Gee, we won't even have time to throw her a shower."

The whole group laughed.

"Seriously, people," Jane said. "I have to get on the ball here. I guess I'll phone Actors' Equity for a tall, dark and handsome guy to fill the bill."

"Mmm," Sue murmured dreamily. "Ask for one for me, too. If he's really good at it, I'll give him a permanent booking."

Jane was running her finger down the list of items in her notebook. "Marsha, you phone Emory Landscapers in Dorset and have them get their very best Scotch pine Christmas tree over to Casey's country place on the double. Oh, and put a call in to a Mrs. Newman—" she barked out the phone number "—and have her give the house a once-over." Jane scribbled on a clean sheet of paper, tore it off and handed it to Sue. "Phone this order into the Dorset General Store to deliver the stuff and leave it in Casey's fridge, as usual. I'm going up there with Casey first thing tomorrow and we'll do a major shopping then."

"Do you have the number?"

"No. You'll have to get it from Vermont information."

Sue glanced at the list and then looked back at Jane. "So, she's having her meeting with Matoki up in her country place?"

Jane gave her a sharp look. "How do you know about Matoki? That was supposed to be hush-hush."

All four women carefully averted their gazes from George. Only Jane's eyes moved in his direction. She smiled wryly, then shrugged. "Before heaven knows what kind of rumors start spreading through the company, you might as well get it right as not. Casey sent Toho Matoki and his wife an invitation to join her for a couple of weeks up at her Vermont farm house to experience a traditional New England Christmas. I have to admit when she sent the invitation I pooh-poohed the idea. She'd been batting zero all year with Matoki."

"Trying to hook up on this new American-style Japanese hotel deal, right?" George asked.

Jane had to laugh. She should have known nothing went down at Hammond that the mail clerk didn't know about.

"Right. And our brilliant young boss finally has her foot in the door. Beating out every other foot. The letter from Matoki arrived today accepting her invitation. And the Matokis arrive in Dorset on Sunday morning. That invitation was a stroke of genius, folks. It dawned on Casey that instead of seducing Matoki with her acquired knowledge of Japanese traditions and negotiating styles, she'd try a whole new angle. Give him a taste of a distinctive American tradition. They do Christmas to perfection in Dorset. I know. My folks have a farmhouse in Ingram, the next town over. I spend Christmas up there every year and we always go over to Dorset. Sleigh rides around the green, carolers at your front door, the shopkeepers dressed in Victorian costumes, apple dunking parties, chestnuts roasting on open fires . . ."

"'Jack Frost nipping at your toes,'" George sang off key.

"Jack Frost, Kris Kringle, the works," Jane summed up. "You'd think you landed smack dab in the middle of a Grandma Moses painting. It's going to wow the Matokis. They're crazy for tradition."

Sue nibbled on the end of her pencil. "I still don't see how Matoki's visit fits in with Croyden needing a husband."

"Elementary, my dear Mintnor," Jane explained. "Matoki thinks Casey is married. When she first made her pitch to Matoki a year ago, she and Carpenter were still together. In the letter we just got from Matoki accepting the invitation, he wrote that he and his wife 'would be honored to share a traditional New England Christmas' with Casey and her 'esteemed husband.'"

George shrugged. "So why not just tell him she's divorced?"

"No can do," Jane said. "Our research boys tell us Matoki is strictly antidivorce. Casey's already got one strike against her being a woman. Matoki has never done a deal with a woman exec before—here, in Japan, anywhere. A divorced woman—well, Casey could just kiss the deal goodbye."

Sue Mintnor echoed Les Rosen's earlier remark. "Do you think she can pull it off?"

Jane raised both hands displaying crossed fingers.

Casey Croyden's door opened for the third time in ten minutes. This time the top exec herself came out. At the sight of the beautiful, blond, five-foot-seven dynamo, the ad hoc coffee klatch—sans their coffee—quickly dispersed and made great efforts to look busy.

Casey cast them all a wry look, then zeroed in on Jane. "Did you make that call yet?"

"Just about to."

She strode briskly over to Jane's desk, several pairs of eyes surrepticiously following her steps. There was a hush. Jane never failed to be impressed by her boss's ability to radiate such sheer mesmerizing energy. It was no easy trick. But, then, Casey Croyden was no ordinary woman.

Casey placed her palms flat on Jane's desk. "Nothing too flashy. Six feet max. Reasonably well built. But definitely no Schwarzenegger types. And no blonds. Eight'll get you ten it'll be a dye job. What I'm looking for...what I want..." Casey shrugged. "You know what I want, Jane.

Just make sure he's not so good-looking he's distracting."

"To you?" Jane querried wryly.

Casey grinned. "To Matoki. Nothing, but nothing, is
going to distract me."

Jane gave Casey a mock salute. "Gotcha, boss."

"Oh, and Jane, he has to be at my place in Dorset by
Saturday evening. That will give me a chance to give him
a rundown on his duties." Casey caught the glint in her
assistant's eye. When she glanced around, she caught the
same glint in the eyes of her two clerks, Marsha and Sue.
Casey grinned. "Shame on all of you. After you take care
of business go wash your mouths out with company
soap." She swung her lithe frame around and headed
back to her office. Before closing the door, she gave Jane
a last admonition. "Remember, I don't want one of those
muscle-bound, glamour-boy types."

As Casey disappeared behind her closed door, she
heard George say, "Hey, Jane, when you call Equity ask
if maybe Danny DeVito would consider the part."

1

On the first day of Christmas...

CASEY WIPED A BEAD of sweat from her forehead, stepped back and examined the newly decorated tree. "It's crooked. It looks like the leaning tree of Dorset."

"The tree's not leaning. It's the floor. This house is close to two hundred years old, Casey," Jane argued, plucking a strand of tinsel from Casey's shoulder-length honey-blond hair. "The tree looks fine. Relax. Come on, let's unpack the groceries. Are you sure you don't want me to try to find someone in town to do the cooking?"

"No. If everything doesn't go perfectly these next twelve days, I don't want to have anyone to blame but myself. Anyway, I'm not a half-bad cook. And with Fanny Farmer, Betty Crocker and *The Joy of Cooking* at my fingertips, what more do I need?"

"Personally," Jane said with a grin, "I'd take *The Joy of Sex* over *The Joy of Cooking* any day."

Casey lifted a brightly painted wooden sled ornament from a low branch and moved it to eye level. "You're sure everything is all set with my new husband?"

Jane's grin broadened at Casey's unconscious connection between *The Joy of Sex* and her "new" husband. "The woman I arranged things with at Actors' Equity promised you'd have no complaints."

Casey stuck the sled back on the bottom branch. "And she said he'd be here by this evening?"

"Check." Jane started off for the kitchen.

"Don't bother with the groceries. I'll put them away after I take a bath. I'm covered with pine needles and tinsel."

"Okay. Anything else you want me to do?"

"No, thanks." Casey gave one last glance around the room. "I've got everything under control."

Jane slipped on her coat and Casey walked her to the front door. It had started snowing. Already a thin blanket of white covered the lawn.

"Great, a white Christmas," Jane said cheerily.

"Unless it turns into a full-fledged blizzard." Casey's forehead creased. "That might affect the Matokis' arrival."

"Nothing wrong with that. It'll just give you more time to get to know your new hubby," Jane pointed out, a twinkle in her eye.

"Really, Jane, I hope this guy works out. If the Matokis ever knew I was pulling the wool over their eyes . . ." She gave a little shiver that had nothing to do with the weather.

"Don't worry. The guy's a professional. And you'll have plenty of time to coach him on his duties," Jane said with a wink. Before heading off she added, "I'll stop by next week on the way to my folks' place in Ingram—just to see how you're making out."

Casey waved goodbye and shut the door. She stripped off her sweatshirt as she climbed the stairs, and was out of the rest of her clothes by the time she got to the bathroom. She started running the tub, let it fill up a bit and poured in some bubble bath. She was just about to step in, when she heard a ringing sound. Her phone or her doorbell? She turned down the taps a little to hear better.

It was her front doorbell. Jane must have gotten halfway down the road and forgotten something, Casey thought, grabbing a bath towel and wrapping it around her.

The doorbell rang for a third time as Casey came running down the stairs. "Hold your horses. I'm coming."

The towel was slipping and she made a grab for it as she opened the door. "Okay, what did you forget?" The last word fell from her lips in a strangled gasp.

A middle-aged Oriental couple stood on the doorstep, polite, matching smiles on their faces, two large leather suitcases at their sides. Casey recognized them instantly from company photos. Her heart sank.

If the Matokis were at all surprised to be greeted by a near-naked hostess, they gave no hint of it. They bowed in unison, little flecks of white snow falling off their shiny black hair.

For several moments, Casey could do nothing but stare in stunned silence at the famous Japanese hotel magnate and his delicately lovely wife.

The Matokis continued to smile, continued to wait, continued to ignore the brief attire of their hostess.

"I . . . I was about to take a bath," Casey said finally. "I didn't . . . I thought . . . I was expecting you . . ."

"Tomorrow," Toho Matoki finished for her, grinning pleasantly, "I know. But you see, a storm was predicted, and since we had arrived in New York City, we thought we'd come early. I did phone, but there was no answer."

"I . . . must have been . . . out shopping."

Mrs. Matoki, a tiny smiling figure in a black wool coat, shivered from the cold. Casey, half-naked at her open door, was too frozen with embarrassment even to realize she was freezing with cold, as well. How could this happen to her? How could the Matokis show up a day early? How could they time their arrival so disastrously? What was she supposed to do now? What was the Japanese word again for welcome? Welcome nothing. What the hell was the Japanese word for help?

"Please, *Croyden-san*," Matoki said politely, using the formal address, "If we are inconveniencing you we would be most happy to find accommodations at an inn for the night."

Casey didn't even hear him. Her mind was racing. "*Irasshai*," she muttered under her breath. Yes, that's it, she thought and said it again, louder. "*Irasshai*. Welcome." She stepped back from the door, started to remove one hand from her towel in a gesture for them to enter, but thought better of it and settled for a motion of her head.

Mr. and Mrs. Matoki bowed and smiled. "*Konnichi-wa*," they murmured in succession, first Toho and then Akiko.

Casey mumbled "*Konnichi-wa*" in return. Good day, indeed!

She stumbled back to allow them to enter. Toho Matoki gathered up both suitcases and walked in first, Akiko coming in behind him. Immediately, as they stepped into the hall, they removed their shoes. Mrs. Matoki bent down and lined them up neatly on the hall rug.

Meanwhile, Casey made a grab for her yellow rain slicker hanging on the brass coat tree. She quickly threw the garment on, making her apologies as she clutched the gaudy colored slicker closed. "I'm so sorry... if only I'd known. I just didn't..."

Mrs. Matoki's smile vanished as she rose from lining up the shoes and turned to face Casey. She gave her a disconcerted look, glanced at her husband, then returned her gaze to Casey. "Please, *Croyden-san.* You have water..."

Casey frowned. "Water? Oh, water. Of course I have water. How thoughtless of me. You must be very thirsty after such a long trip. But wouldn't you prefer tea? It'll only take a couple of minutes. Let me make you both a nice pot of tea." She saw that they didn't look particularly pleased by the suggestion. American, more American. "Or perhaps you'd like coffee. I grind the beans myself. I get them at this incredibly quaint little general store in town. It won't take a minute..."

"No, please, *Croyden-san,*" Mrs. Matoki said more insistently, casting her eyes just beyond her hostess. "You misunderstand. Water..."

Casey raised a hand in immediate acquiescence. "Water. Absolutely. Nice tall glasses of water. Whatever you like. Really. Please come inside to the living room and make yourselves comfortable. I'll get a nice pitcher of water for you and then I'll...make myself presentable."

Casey started to lead the way to the living room, only to discover after five steps that the Matokis weren't following. She turned to find the pair standing exactly where she'd left them, looks of mild consternation on both their faces. Casey swallowed. What bit of arcane Japanese protocol had she forgotten? Was she supposed to show them up to their rooms first? But hadn't they asked, most insistently, for water? Did they want her to bring their drinks to their rooms? Was there some Japanese pre-water-drinking ritual they partook in?

Casey gave them a helpless look. The look they returned matched hers. Finally, Mrs. Matoki pointed hesitantly in the direction of the staircase.

Casey quickly nodded. Yes, that was it. "Of course. You'd like to go to your rooms, freshen up first. I can bring a pitcher of water right up to you, if you like," she hastily offered.

Mrs. Matoki's delicate hand went to her lips.

Toho Matoki's expression grew stern. "You are having a problem, *Croyden-san*."

"Please, call me 'Casey.' And don't worry. There's no problem. I know I must seem a little . . . flustered . . . but, honestly, everything is going to be fine. Really. Why don't I just show you to your rooms, get the water . . ."

"Yes, the water, *Croyden-san* . . . Casey. Please," he said most earnestly, his right hand motioning toward the staircase. "Look for yourself."

Befuddled, Casey's eyes followed his lead. She gasped in horror. And then the light finally dawned. "Oh, my God, the tub. I . . . I left the tub on. I forgot . . ." She stood frozen to the spot, mesmerized by the steady stream of foaming, bubbly water cascading down the steps.

"Perhaps," Toho suggested, "you should . . ."

Casey shook herself. "Of course. Please, just . . . just don't worry about a thing. No problem. I'll take care of everything," she muttered as she hurried to the stairs. Halfway up, she waved back down to the Matokis, who remained standing in the front hall, watching her ascent. "No problem. It's only water. I'll have it fixed in a jiffy. Be right back."

She hurried up the rest of the stairs, coming close to catastrophe when the towel she still had wrapped around her under the slicker came undone and dropped to her feet. She tripped on it, felt herself losing her balance, made a frantic grab for the banister and only barely kept herself from tumbling backward down the stairs. Once she was sure of her footing, she made it up the last two steps, waved again down to the Matokis, who hadn't moved. Mrs. Matokis hand was still pressed against her lips. "I'm fine. Everything's fine."

The bathroom floor was a sea of bubbles. Casey waded in, shut the door and sank to her knees on the tile floor, landing in a couple of inches of soapsuds. Her hands were trembling as she turned off the taps. A wave of soapy water splashed down the front of her slicker as she stuck her hand in the tub to remove the rubber stopper from the drain.

She stayed put on her knees, too distraught to rise. Her chin dropped to her chest, her eyes started to tear, and when she reached for a sheet of toilet paper to blow her nose, the whole roll popped out of its holder and landed in the puddle of water.

Casey sank to a sitting position, knees pulled up to her chest. How was she going to go down there and face the man who held her future in his hands, after she'd made such an utter fool of herself? A practically naked utter fool, no less.

How had she gotten as far as she had in this cutthroat business? Not by accident. And not by accepting defeat. *No*, she told herself. *I will not let one little catastrophe ruin everything I've worked so hard for.* She lifted her chin, threw her shoulders back and snatched the two bath towels off the rack to soak up the soapsuds and water on the floor. The whole time she sopped, wrung out the towels and sopped some more, she was muttering hotly to herself, "Great Casey. Just great. Oh, *Matoki-san*, you want water, not tea. Of course, water. I'll get you water. No problem. All the water you want." She sighed deeply. "No problem."

She sniffed, rose to her feet and surveyed the damage. The heavy, absorbent towels had done a reasonably thorough job of soaking up most of the mess. Casey decided she'd better put on some clothes before she toweled up the sudsy water in the upstairs hall and on the staircase.

Five minutes later, dressed in a dry skirt and sweater, her hair combed, a dab of lipstick on, Casey felt almost normal, almost as if she had things under control.

Until she walked out of her room and got to the top of the stairs, only to find Mr. and Mrs. Matoki both still in their coats, on their knees, working their way up the steps, busily sopping up water with paper toweling.

"No. No, please. Don't. Please, you're my guests. I'll do that. I'll—" Casey was so frantic she never gave it a thought that the top steps were still wet. Wet and especially slippery from the bubble bath.

As Casey came thumping down the stairs on her bottom, Mrs. Matoki let out a cry of alarm and stepped aside, while the thin, small-framed Mr. Matoki did his best to halt Casey's descent.

He let out a whoosh of air as she crashed into him, and he slid down the last three steps with her, both of them coming to a resounding final thump on the hall floor.

It was the last straw for Casey. Tears sprang to her eyes and she started to cry. She hadn't cried in front of anyone since she was twelve.

The poor Matokis looked at the crying woman in alarm, thinking she must have seriously injured herself. Mr. Matoki, unhurt by the fall, got to his knees and anxiously asked her where she was hurt. Mrs. Matoki hurried to Casey's asistance, as well. Through her tears, Casey tried to assure them she was fine. "Just fine." She was worried about Mr. Matoki, but he assured her he was "just fine" too.

Mr. and Mrs. Matoki each gripped one of Casey's arms and helped her up. At five-foot-seven, Casey stood a good six inches over Mrs. Matoki and probably close to four inches over Mr. Matoki. She stared down at them, sniffed back her tears and made a concerted effort to smile. Eagerly, gladly, they smiled back at her.

Mrs. Matoki clasped her hands together. "Now, perhaps, we can all have a pot of tea. Yes, tea would be very nice, Casey. You must rest from your fall and allow me...."

"Oh, no, no." Casey smoothed down her skirt, wiped her damp cheeks. "Honestly I'm fine. I'm just so embarrassed. Please, the least I can do for you is make the tea." She tried to sound composed, tried for a smile.

Toho Matoki patted her arm. "Don't feel embarrassed, Casey. Why, tomorrow we will all look back on this and laugh." There was a definite twinkle in his eye.

Casey started to feel better. Maybe everything would work out, after all. She took the Matokis' coats and hung them up on the hall tree. Then, with a little spring in her step, she led the way into the living room.

"Such a lovely room," Mrs. Matoki said, taking in the large living room with its knotty pine walls, braided rugs scattered on the pine floors, the large brick hearth and the worn fruitwood furniture that bore the patina of fine antiques. "Did you have a decorator," she asked, "or did you and your husband do it yourselves?"

Husband? Husband! Oh, no, Casey thought in a panic. Her husband. She'd forgotten all about her husband. The Matokis were probably wondering where he was. It was Saturday, so he wouldn't be at work. Okay, okay, that was no problem. She could simply tell them he was off doing...doing errands. The real problem was that he would be arriving sometime this evening, and she wouldn't have any time to warn him that he was going to have to step right on stage and start performing with no rehearsal.

Casey's mind raced as she continued to stare blankly at Akiko Matoki. Akiko gave her husband a worried look.

"Are you all right, Casey," Toho asked with concern.

"It's my husband..." The words popped out of her mouth.

"Your husband?" Akiko Matoki smiled at Casey encouragingly. "You mean your husband did the decorating?"

"No. Yes. I mean... I was just thinking about him."

"Oh?"

"He's not home."

The Matokis looked at each other, then back at Casey. "Yes," Toho said. "That's all right."

"He's off at the..." Casey started to say supermarket, but then he'd be expected to arrive home with groceries. "At the... lumberyard. Putting in an order. A building project."

"Is that right?" Toho seemed interested.

"Yes. Yes, he's so... handy. With his hands." She shut her eyes. *Oh, great, Casey. You're doing just great.*

"I'm not so bad with my hands, either," Toho said with a smile.

"Yes," Akiko piped in. "My husband is a fine carpenter, Casey."

"And you say your husband has a building project he is planning? Then, while we're visiting, perhaps I can help."

Casey swallowed hard. For all she knew her "husband" couldn't tell one end of a hammer from the other. "Well, it's still... in the planning stages. He won't actually do any building until . . . the spring. The ground, you know. It's so hard."

"What exactly is he building?" Toho asked.

"What is he building? Well, it's a . . . shed. A new shed. For, you know, the lawn mower."

"But you have such a big barn beside your house," Akiko pointed out.

"Yes, it is big. Big . . . but, not very sturdy. Oh, I mean, nothing to worry about."

Toho smiled. "I'm not worried. Akiko and I have looked forward to experiencing a truly unique New England Christmas. We are sure we'll have a wonderful time."

"Well," Casey muttered, "I'm definitely making it unique for you." She sighed. "I'll fix the tea."

AFTER THEY HAD THEIR TEA, Casey showed the Matokis to their rooms, a large, rose-and-cream-papered bedroom with its canopied bed, large pine wardrobe and chintz sofa. Adjoining the bedroom was a cozy sitting room and bath. The suite was on the east side of the house, right next to the bedroom Casey usually slept in. For this occasion, however, Casey was staying at the other end of the house in a bedroom that had a small nursery attached to it. The arrangement would allow Casey to keep up the appearance of sleeping with her "husband," while he actually slept on the divan in the nursery.

The Matokis decided to take a brief rest before dinner. Casey prayed that her husband would show up while her guests were upstairs, so that she'd at least be able to give him some warning that opening night had been moved up. Meanwhile the snowfall had turned into a full-scale blizzard, and Casey began panicking that good old hubby wouldn't be able to make it up there from New York at all. Why did she have to think up such a dumb excuse for his absence as going to the lumberyard? She could have easily said he was in New York on business. Sure, if she was thinking straight.

The doorbell rang at six-fifteen. With a mixture of relief and anxiety, Casey raced from the living room hoping the sound wouldn't awaken the Matokis.

Casey flung the door open, frowning as she grabbed hold of the snow-covered man standing on the doorstep. Hadn't she specifically told Jane not too handsome? Well, at least he wasn't blond.

"Thank goodness you made it," she exclaimed, grabbing hold of his sleeve and pulling him through the doorway. "I started to panic what with this storm and all. You're never going to believe this. They're here. Upstairs."

Once she had the actor inside the hall, she had a chance to get a better look at him. Her frown deepened. He was too good-looking by half. He just barely came in under the required six feet max. And while the square-jawed face was a bit too rugged to be Hollywood handsome, it was definitely Hollywood sexy. Not the muscle-bound, glamour-boy type, though. He was grittier. There was more character in his face. Clark Gable without the mustache. Casey never much cared for mustaches.

She would have preferred a blander sort. But the age was right, mid-thirties, she guessed. And he had a classy manner, a definite style. Matoki might be impressed by that. Anyway, Casey thought, she was in no position to complain. He'd have to do.

She saw that he was giving her a close survey to match her own, his expression puzzled.

"The agency was supposed to fill you in a little. You know about the Matokis?"

"The Matokis?" Now he frowned. "Look, I just—"

"Shhh. Not so loud."

"Sorry. Can I just . . . ?"

"There's no time. . . ."

"But . . ."

They both heard the footsteps on the stairs. Before her new husband could say another word, Casey threw her arms around his neck. "Darling, I'm so glad you're back safely." In a low whisper, she added. "Quick, what's your name?"

"Uh . . . John. John Gallagher."

"It's John Croyden now," she breathed against his ear. "John," she said in a louder voice, "guess what? The Matokis have arrived a day early. Isn't that wonderful? I told them you'd be back from the lumberyard before dinner." Her arms still around John's neck, she glanced around and pretended to just now spot Mrs. Matoki on the stairs.

"Oh, Akiko . . ." She swiveled her head back round to John. "Akiko Matoki, darling." Her arms moved from his neck to the front of his coat. "Come, take off your coat. Let me introduce you. And you probably want a cocktail. Your usual martini."

John gave her a baffled look. "My usual martini?"

"Just the way you like it." She manufactured a shrill little laugh as she began to unbutton John's coat.

He tried to stop her. "Don't . . ."

"Sorry, darling. You do it yourself." She smiled over at Akiko, who was slowly coming down the stairs. No doubt, the poor woman didn't want to risk a repeat of Casey's unorthodox method of descent.

"Akiko, come meet my husband, John." Before she got the words out she saw Toho Matoki at the top of the stairs. "Oh . . . good . . . you're both up from your naps. See, Toho, I told you my husband would make it back before dinner. Let me introduce you both." She glanced back at John. "Darling, take off your coat." Under her breath, she whispered, "Hurry up."

John's hand went to his top button. "I'm a little confused..."

Casey laughed gaily. "It's all right, darling. You see the Matokis were worried about the storm affecting their travel plans, so they came today, instead. Isn't that wonderful? And really, they've been so understanding about my... my not being completely prepared." She was working at his buttons as she spoke, and practically yanked the coat off of him.

The Matokis stood side by side in the hall and smiled politley at the tall, attractive man. "We are most honored, *Croydon-san.*"

"'John,'" Casey piped in. "Call him 'John.'"

Akiko raised a thin black eyebrow. "John."

"Yes. Well, 'Jonathan,'" Casey said nervously. "But I prefer...'John.' John...prefers 'John,' too. Right, John?"

John grinned. "Yes, I definitely prefer 'John' to 'Jonathan.'"

Casey smiled with relief. "See. Now we have that much cleared up." She shoved her hand in the crook of John's arm. "Now let's all go into the living room and have a drink before dinner." John was reluctant to move. She couldn't blame him. Clearly the man hadn't been coached at all. At a loss for what else to do, she threw her arms around him again. "Oh, I'm just so glad you made it home safely in this storm." In a low voice she instructed, "Just follow my lead. I'll explain everything later. Please..."

John pulled his head back and gave Casey an assessing look. What he saw he definitely liked. Honey-blond hair falling in cascading waves to her shoulders, azure blue eyes, dynamite bone structure, and from the feel of her pressing against him, a dynamite body to match. He smiled approvingly. Casey's big blue eyes reflected pure gratitude. She placed her hand back in the crook of his arm, and before he could say or do anything that would give the whole charade away, she pulled him down the hall in the direction of the living room, the Matokis following.

"You will help me with dinner, darling?" She glanced over her shoulder to the Matokis. "John's a wonderful cook."

"Not really," John muttered.

"He's so modest."

"And I understand, John, you're a fine carpenter, as well." Toho added.

"I am?"

"See," Casey jumped in. "I told you. Modest to a fault."

"Ah, you must be quite adept at the craft to be undertaking the building of a large shed," Toho commented.

John looked at Casey. "A shed?"

She squeezed his arm hard. "I forgot. You don't call it a shed." She smiled back at the Matokis. "He doesn't call it a shed. He calls it a . . ." She came to a halt as she tried to think up something else to call it. The others stopped with her and waited.

John was smiling at her. It was a very distracting smile. "What do I call it, darling?"

"A . . . a hut." Her smile looked pained. "Quaint."

"Yes," Akiko agreed. "Everything is so quaint in New England. And your house so lovely, John. And Casey tells me you helped to decorate it. A man of many talents."

"Well, now...Akiko...I never really looked at it that way before," John mused.

Akiko smiled sweetly at Casey and gave Toho's hand a little squeeze. "How lucky we are to each have such talented husbands."

Casey stretched her frozen smile. "Yes. Lucky. So lucky."

They continued on to the living room, but as they approached the entry, John turned to Casey. "Can I have a word with you in the kitchen . . . darling?"

"Absolutely." She turned to the Matokis. "Do you mind? We'll only be a minute. I've got a fire going. Just relax. We'll be right back."

"Excuse me, Casey," Akiko broke in. "I was looking for my purse."

"Oh, it's probably on the hall table by the door. Let me get it for you."

"I can do it."

They both started for the front hall as the doorbell rang.

Casey scowled. "I can't imagine who that could be. I'm not expecting anyone else."

"Perhaps someone's auto is stranded in the snow," Toho suggested.

"Yes," Casey agreed, "That must be it."

As Casey went to see who was ringing the bell, the others remained in the hall watching her.

She started to open the door cautiously and then felt it being shoved open the rest of the way. Before she could utter a word, the strange man standing on the doorstep moved swiftly inside the house, threw his arms passionately around the dumbfounded Casey, smiled at the group at the end of the hall and said in a loud and resonant voice for all to hear, "Sorry, sweetheart, I forgot my house key."

2

Deck the halls with boughs of holly...

THE STRANGER KEPT ONE ARM firmly entrenched around Casey and waved with his free hand to the threesome standing down the hall.

"Who are you?" Casey whispered in his ear.

"David Quinn. Actors' Equity," the man whispered back to Casey. "Who's the other guy?"

"My husband," she muttered under her breath.

"But I thought . . . you hired two husbands?" he muttered back.

Casey's head was spinning. She cast the Matokis and husband number one a wan smile. *Come on, Casey. You've had to think on your feet before.* "Oh . . . look who's here. What . . . a nice . . . surprise."

The Matokis and John Gallagher smiled back expectantly.

"It's . . . my brother." She gulped, then gave the actor a squeeze. "My brother . . . David."

"Brother?" The actor mumbled. "But I thought . . ."

"Don't think." She managed the order without moving her lips.

"It's your show." David picked up his suitcase, brought it in the hall and closed the door.

Casey sighed. Her show, indeed. John Gallagher walked over, the Matokis coming up behind him.

"Nice to . . . see you, David." John extended his hand to the actor, then gave Casey an amused smile. "Why, Casey and I were talking about you just yesterday, weren't we, darling?"

"Huh? Oh . . . yes. Yes, we were." She stared at John Gallagher with a baffled expression. Wait a minute. Hold everything. If John Gallagher wasn't her hired husband then . . . who the hell was he?

"How nice," Akiko said with a bright smile. "A family reunion, yes?"

Casey's stomach was doing somersaults. "A reunion. It is nice . . . isn't it?"

Toho seemed pleased, as well, with the arrival of Casey's "brother." "So, has it been a while, then, since you and your sister have seen each other?"

David cast Casey a baffled glare. Quickly she piped up with, "Months. Several months. Three months. Maybe . . . four. David lives in . . . Philadelphia."

Toho looked puzzled. "But that isn't so very far from New York City."

"No," Casey concurred. "No, it isn't very far. But . . . it's . . ."

John Gallagher came to the rescue. "It's David's work. He's on the road a lot. You're still regional sales manager for that plastics company, aren't you, David?"

"Right," Quinn said amiably. Brother, husband . . . as long as the pay was the same he really had no gripe.

"Let me take your coat. And then we can all go into the living room," John said with a big smile. "We were just about to have drinks, weren't we, darling?"

"Drinks? Oh, yes . . . right."

John had already hung David's coat on the coat tree in the hall and was leading the way into the living room. Toho Matoki walked alongside David, asking him more about his work. Akiko smiled at Casey as they followed the men. "You must be very happy to have your brother here. I think the two of you must be close. And your husband...he likes your brother, too. That's good. Family is so important, don't you think?"

Casey smiled wanly. "Yes. I couldn't agree more."

John was at the bar, playing host. A damn charming host at that. Even now, Casey had to admit Gallagher was doing a great job. The question was, why was he doing such a good job? And who *was* John Gallagher?

Casey remained at the entry to the living room. "Oh, John...dear. You were going to help me with...the hors d'oeurvres...in the kitchen, remember?"

John finished pouring a Scotch over rocks for Toho. "Coming. Help yourself, David. You know your way around."

Casey couldn't take her eyes off John as he crossed the living room and came toward her. Who the hell was he? What was she doing thinking that he was really perfect for the part of her husband? This wasn't his part. Only now it seemed it was. This was turning out to be the very worst day of her life.

John came up to her and smiled. "Relax, sweetheart. It'll be okay."

And then, before Casey could say anything, he swept her into his arms and planted a most "husbandly" kiss on her lips.

When he released her she was reeling. "What... why...?" Would she ever be coherent again? At the moment she doubted it. At the moment she was doubting just about everything. Everything except that this impossible stranger's kiss was having a devastating effect on her.

He grinned, pointing an index finger over her head. "Mistletoe, darling."

"Oh," She caught Akiko Matoki's shy smile. "Mistletoe," she called out inanely. "It's an old custom. Kissing. Under mistletoe. Tradition."

Akiko laughed softly. "Very nice." She gave her husband a sly look. He grinned at her.

Casey's legs were rubbery as she led John into the kitchen. As soon as they got there, she closed the door and leaned weakly against it.

"Okay, mister. What's your game?"

John laughed. "Shouldn't that be my line, darling?"

Casey frowned. "You aren't the man I hired to play my husband."

"No. That's true. I'm not the man you hired to play your husband. And frankly, darling, I can't imagine why anyone with your looks and class couldn't get a husband for free."

"Very funny, Mr. Gallagher. And you can stop with the darlings."

"Cheer up, Casey. Obviously you made a mistake, jumped to the wrong conclusion and—"

"And," she said hotly, "you played right along. You led me to believe . . . you acted . . ."

"If you recall, darling . . ." He grinned. "Sorry, it just slipped out. Where was I? Oh, yes. If you recall, Casey, you didn't exactly give me any opportunity to explain. I ring your doorbell and the next thing I know you're throwing your arms around me in a passionate embrace."

"I thought you were my husband. I mean . . . I thought you were the man I hired. I thought you were David."

"You mean your brother?"

Casey pressed her palms to her temples. "My head is spinning."

John put an arm around her shoulder. "Come on and sit down. Tell hubby all about it."

Casey was too upset to balk. She sat at the kitchen table and rested her head in her cupped hands. After a couple of moments she raised her head and looked at John, who had taken a seat beside her. "Who are you? What were you doing at my front door?"

He shifted a few inches closer to her. "I'm your next-door neighbor. I rented the Foster place for the holidays. When I arrived I discovered there was something wrong with the boiler. No heat. No hot water. Oh, and no telephone. I saw your lights on, so I came over to ask if I could use your phone."

"My telephone?" A strand of her honey-blond hair fell over her right eyes. John reached out and tenderly smoothed it back into place.

"Is it all right?"

Casey stared at him dumbly.

"Can I use your phone? To call a plumber?"

Casey nodded morosely. The worst scenario that could happen had happened. There was nothing left for her to do but come clean to Matoki and then...and then commit hari-kari.

As Casey sat at the kitchen table postponing the inevitable, John started dialing the brief list of plumbers in the phone book. There was no answer at the first number. Then he tried Mullen's Plumbing and Heating and got a recorded message saying they were closed for the holidays. The final call was to a surly plumber who wasn't taking any new jobs until after the New Year.

"Now what do I do?" John muttered as he hung up the phone.

Casey had been so lost in her own worries, she hadn't been paying much attention to John's plight. "What's the matter?"

"I can't get anyone to come out. And I've never fixed a boiler in my life. I don't think I'm going to have much luck with it. I don't suppose you know anything about boilers."

Casey was staring hard at him, but she wasn't listening to a word he was saying about his heating problem. She was too busy solving her own problems. "Wait a minute. Of course. Why wouldn't it work?"

John scowled. "Why wouldn't what work?"

"You can't stay next door. You'll freeze to death. You can stay here, instead. Oh John, you don't know what it would mean to me. You'd be saving my life. Well, my career, anyway. You see, if I have to tell Matoki I've been conning him about a husband, I can kiss my future goodbye. And really, it's so simple. I need a husband desperately. And you need a place to stay. Well, we'd have to keep up the pretense of being married, but I've got a perfectly lovely room right off my bedroom where you can stay. And I promise I'll do everything possible to make you comfortable. Oh, John, I know you don't know me from Adam and there isn't a reason in the world for you to go along with this charade for me . . . but I'd make it worth your while."

"Oh?"

"I mean . . . I'd gladly pay you. Three hundred a day. Two weeks. That's thirty-six hundred dollars."

"That's quite a lot of money. Especially as I assume you're already paying your . . . uh-mmm . . . brother out there that fee?"

"Let me worry about my finances. Believe me, if I can pull this off, it'll more than make up for the loss."

"What's the deal? Who is this Matoki? And how come you need a husband?"

Casey gave him a thumbnail sketch of the situation.

"I see the problem," John said after listening intently. "But wouldn't it have been better to . . ."

"To what? Tell Matoki I've divorced? I could kiss the deal goodbye for sure. You don't know Matoki."

"Actually, I do. I mean I know the type. You see, I've spent some time in Japan and I've met fellows like Matoki before. Real sticklers for tradition. And honor."

Casey nodded glumly. "Maybe hari-kari is the answer." She looked up at him. "How come you were in Japan?"

"I did some consulting work for an American fast-food chain that was branching out to the Japanese market. General Lee's Fried Chicken. They're doing quite well out there."

"How nice for you."

John smiled gently. "You really are in a jam, aren't you?"

Casey gave him a beseeching look. "You could save my life."

"Your career," he corrected.

"My career is my life."

"It shouldn't be that way."

"I know. Look, as my husband, you can lecture me till doomsday. Or at least for the next two weeks. Just say you'll stay. Say you'll pretend to be my husband. I know it's a lot to ask, but you are sort of in a jam yourself. No heat. No hot water. No plumber. And I happen to know the Fosters have had trouble with their chimney and so you'd be taking a risk using the fireplace. And . . . and there's a full-scale blizzard going on outside. The roads are treacherous. You wouldn't be able to travel in this

weather. I mean...I'd feel personally responsible if...if
anything were to happen to you. If you skidded off the
road, got stranded, crashed into a tree." She stopped for
a second to catch her breath. "Oh, John, please say yes."

"That's quite a proposal, Casey."

"Does that mean . . . you will?"

"I wish I could, Casey. Something tells me you'd make
some lucky fellow a terrific wife."

"But . . . but, why can't you?" she persisted. "What
possible reason—?" Before she could finish, the doorbell rang. Again. Casey's mouth dropped open and she
stared at John in horror. "Oh, no. No. I can't take any
more catastrophes. If this is another husband . . ." The
doorbell rang again, several times in succession. "That's
crazy. I've got to get a grip on myself." She rose, taking
hold of John's arm. "Look, don't go away. I know we can
work out some sort of deal. Whatever reservations or
concerns you have—" There were three more rings. "Just
stay put. I'll be right back."

When she got into the hall, she saw David Quinn
starting for the door. "That's okay. I'll get it. Tell the
Matokis I'll be with them in . . . in a few minutes."

David gave a nervous nod and withdrew. Casey hurried to the door, relieved to find, upon opening it, a
young woman rather than yet another "husband"
standing there. The woman was an attractive brunette.
Attractive and chilled.

"Excuse me. I'm Brenda Gallagher and I was wondering if . . ."

"Gallagher?" Casey's heart sank.

"Yes. And I . . ."

"You're staying next door?"

"Why, yes. You see there's no heat and John said he'd come over here to use your phone. He's been gone so long, though . . ."

"You aren't John's sister, I suppose?" Casey asked with a wilting voice.

"His sister?" The attractive Brenda Gallagher laughed. "Hardly."

"I didn't think so." Casey stepped away from the door. "He's here. In the kitchen. This way..." Casey started off, looking much like a mourner on her way to a funeral. She was. Her own.

"Has he found a plumber, then?" Brenda asked as she followed along beside Casey.

"No. No, he hasn't."

"Oh, dear. Now what do we do?"

Casey stopped in her tracks. Wait a sec. All wasn't lost yet. She swung abruptly round to face Brenda. "Look, I was just telling your husband I have the perfect solution to your problem. You can stay here...both of you. With me. As my guests. It's a huge house."

"Oh . . . we couldn't." Brenda demurred.

Casey took her arm. "No really. You'd be doing me a favor."

"I would?"

"You *and* John. Mr. Gallagher. Your husband. It's a bit complicated. Come on into the kitchen and I'll explain everything."

"TOHO, AKIKO, I'd like you to meet a dear friend of mine, Brenda Gallagher." Casey put an affectionate arm around the woman as they entered the living room after an earnest five-minute powwow in the kitchen. "We go way back, don't we, Brenda?"

"Way back," Brenda agreed, giving the Matokis bright smiles and then turning that smile on David Quinn, who continued to wear a baffled expression. It wasn't that he was unwilling to go along with changes in the script. It was not having any script at all. He really wasn't very good at improvisation.

Brenda walked over to the actor. "Hi David. Good to see you again. It's been ages. Positively ages."

David shrugged. "I guess it has."

Casey was worried about David. He looked as though he wasn't having an easy time of it. But as for Brenda Gallagher, once John had convinced her to help out, she'd been a terrific sport about the whole charade.

John called out from the hall. "Come help me finish up with the hors d'oeuvres, darling."

Casey shot Brenda an awkward look, wondering how the woman felt about her husband calling another woman "darling" with such *élan*. And Casey wondered guiltily how Brenda would have felt if she'd witnessed the kiss she and John had shared under the mistletoe.

"Go ahead, Casey," Brenda said warmly. "You know how John is in the kitchen." She grinned at the Matokis. "All thumbs, our John."

"Ah, but Casey has told us," commented Toho, "that her husband was quite skilled in the kitchen. And in carpentry, as well."

Uh-oh, Casey thought, catching Brenda's startled look. Don't blow it now . . . please.

"Carpentry? You mean hammer and nails. Yes, John is handy. Building things. And," Brenda said with a casual shrug, "I suppose he probably has improved in the culinary department."

"Oh, yes," Casey piped in a bit breathlessly, smiling gratefully at Brenda. "Really, you wouldn't believe how good he is . . . at cooking."

"Well," Brenda said with an impish smile, "I suppose I really don't know John all that well."

Casey took a couple of steps back. "Still, I'd better make sure he doesn't forget to pop the cheese puffs in the oven."

"Go ahead, Casey. Your brother and I will look after your guests." Brenda had already turned to Toho. "Casey tells me you are in the hotel business in Japan. I once stayed in a marvelous Japanese hotel in Tokyo. The Kimura, I believe it was called."

Toho beamed. "One of mine. A particular favorite."

As Casey returned to the kitchen, she was doing something that just ten minutes ago she wouldn't have dreamed would be possible. She was smiling.

John observed her closely as she came over to help him finish putting together the cheese puffs. She felt flustered by the intensity of his gaze and she was still flustered by the reaction she'd had to his kiss. On top of everything else, he was a married man. He had no business kissing her like that. He had no business playing his part that well. And Casey certainly had no business feeling as attracted to him as she had been feeling.

Finally, after being unable to tolerate his lengthy study any longer, she said, "What is it? Why are you looking at me that way?"

He smiled rakishly. "You should see your face."

Automatically her palms went to her cheeks. She felt their warmth. "What's . . . wrong with my face?"

His smile deepened, laugh lines creasing the corners of his eyes. He took hold of her wrists, gently drawing her hands down from her face. "Nothing," he murmured. "Absolutely nothing's wrong with your face."

Casey knew the rosy hue in her cheeks was deepening.

"Oh..."

She saw him edge closer, knew that he was going to kiss her again. This time it wouldn't be for any audience. There was no reason...

"Don't, John. This is impossible. How can you...? You're a...married man."

He made no effort to back off. Casey could feel his warm breath on her face. "I know. And this is our honeymoon."

Casey felt truly stricken with guilt. "Your honeymoon?" she gasped. "Oh, no."

"And yours."

Casey stared at him angrily. "That isn't what I meant and you know it. I'm talking about poor Brenda out there."

"Believe me, she's not poor."

"Oh, I see. You think because you provide her with a few luxuries you can...can carry on with other women as you please? Men."

"Hold on, darling. You did the proposing here, not me."

"And you intend to take full advantage of the situation, is that it?"

"Why, darling, I do believe we're having our first marital spat."

"How can you be so glib, John? How long have you and Brenda been married, anyway?"

"A couple of years."

"Then you still are practically in the honeymoon stage."

"Believe me, we've definitely left the honeymoon behind."

"You . . . have?" Casey looked down, saw the firmness of his arms where he'd rolled up his shirt cuffs. His hand moved to take her chin.

"Casey, you have a frustrating habit of jumping to conclusions. Do you realize that?"

"I do?" She couldn't meet his gaze.

"Brenda and I are divorced."

"Divorced? But . . ."

"We were married for two years, and we've been divorced for nearly a year."

Casey gave him a wary look. "You might have told me before."

"When? You rushed Brenda in here, begged us to go along with your scam and then dragged Brenda out to introduce her to the Matokis."

"I guess I didn't give you much of a chance. But you deliberately led me on just now."

John looked duly contrite. "That was wrong. I'm sorry. I should have told you straight out. Will you forgive me?"

Casey wasn't exactly in any position to carry a grudge. Besides, she hadn't altogether objected to his flirtatious playfulness. He definitely had a way about him, this John Gallagher.

Still, she continued to eye him warily. "If you and Brenda are divorced, what are the two of you doing up here together?"

"It's all perfectly innocent, I swear. I needed a few weeks away and so I rented the Foster place for the holidays. A couple of days ago, Brenda called and wanted to go over a business investment portfolio that we still hold in common. We both agreed it was time to reorganize, divvy up the investments. So, I suggested she come up to Dorset for a couple of days to go over everything. Strictly a business get-together. You have no cause for jealousy, darling," he teased.

"I'm not jealous. Simply curious, that's all."

His hand was no longer cupping her chin. It had moved to the spot where her neck curved into her shoulder.

His light touch was making her dizzy. "It ... explains ... why Brenda was so agreeable about letting me borrow you to play my husband."

"I'm no longer hers to lend, Casey."

She could feel his hand tighten on her shoulder. She could smell the freshness of his starched shirt, the citrusy scent of his after-shave. She could feel herself wanting to reach for him, pull him closer. She could feel herself being drawn to him like a plant to sunlight.

Wait, she forced herself to think, *wait. This is no time to lose control.* This is no time to let what could only be called a precarious charade slide over into an even more hazardous reality. She desperately needed to keep everything under tight control. John Gallagher threatened that control. On the other hand, she had to admit, without his cooperation there was no control at all.

"What's the matter, Casey? Is it really so terrible to feel attracted to me?"

"I'm not ... I can't be ... I don't want to be ..."

"I'm attracted to you, too."

"No, John. This can't be part of the deal. It's complicated enough. And to be frank, I've sworn off men since Wes."

"Wes?"

"My real husband. My ex-husband, that is. We've been divorced for six months. Actually, we've gotten along better since the divorce than we ever did while we were married."

"Kind of like me and Brenda. What's Wes do?"

"He's a travel photographer for a Boston paper."

"And since Wes . . . no one?"

"No one," Casey said firmly. "And that's the way I want it."

"Is it really, Casey?"

She gave him a beseeching look. "Please, John. Don't make this any harder for me than it already is. I started off with the Matokis and one fake husband. And now I've got a fake husband, a fake brother, a fake childhood girlfriend . . ." She could feel tears threatening. "Why is this happening to me?"

He smiled. The smile was so warm, so tender and yet so provocative that it took Casey's breath away.

"I'm afraid it's happening to me, too," he whispered. He couldn't take his eyes off her face. A perfectly modeled face with perfectly sculpted features. Not a flaw to be found. His hand reached out for hers. His thumb slowly rubbed the back of her hand.

"Oh, this is awful."

"Awful?" He leaned closer, his free hand finding its way to the side of her face. He smoothed back a wave of honey-colored hair. "It can't be awful to feel this good."

"It . . . can't?" She had trouble getting the words out. Her heart was pounding. It was becoming difficult to breathe normally.

His eyes held her captive as he tilted her head up and found her lips. His kiss was soft, firm, tender and demanding all at once. She really couldn't help kissing him back . . . just a little.

"Am I interrupting a rehearsal?"

At the sound of Brenda's voice, Casey and John jumped, Casey practically knocking John down as she shoved him away. Her cheeks were burning.

John merely laughed. "Your timing is impeccable, Bren."

"Sorry about that," she said with wry amusement.

"No, I'm sorry," Casey said, mortified. "I don't know what's gotten into me. I just . . ."

"Take it easy, Casey," Brenda said pleasantly, and then gave John a stern look. "Haven't you told her yet? You are still an impossible tease, John."

"Not guilty," John said, smiling. "Casey knows we're divorced."

"Well, then," Brenda said airily, "no problem."

Brenda's casual acceptance of the situation only increased Casey's discomfort. "The cheese puffs . . ." she mumbled, grabbing the tray from the counter.

"I think you better forget about the cheese puffs for the moment," Brenda said, a note of caution in her voice.

"Why?" Casey was almost afraid to hear the answer.

"A car just pulled up out front. I took a peek and saw a man taking a suitcase out of the trunk.

Casey started to sway. John grabbed her just in the knick of time.

"Was it . . . a red . . . sports car?" Casey's voice was a shaky whisper.

Brenda nodded. "Is that bad?"

Casey sank limply against John. "Wes."

Brenda cast John a puzzled look. "Wes?"

Before John could fill Brenda in, the kitchen door swung open and a tall, burly snow-covered man filled the entry.

"Hi, babe. What gives? I wasn't expecting a party."

Casey could do nothing for several moments but stare. Finally she asked, "What are you doing here? How did you . . . get in?"

"A sweet-looking little Oriental lady let me in," Wes said cheerily. "Who is she?"

"Oh, no. No. Tell me this is all some horrible nightmare," Casey moaned.

Wes wore a perplexed expression. "Hey, Case. I'm sorry. I just thought . . . you always told me I could use the place if I needed to get away for a couple of days. I didn't think you'd be here. I certainly didn't know you'd be having a housefull of guests."

Casey continued to stare at Wes in horror. "What . . . what did you tell her?"

"Her?"

"Akiko Matoki."

"The one who opened—"

"Yes. Yes."

"Nothing. I didn't tell her anything. Well, my name. And then I asked where you were."

"You're sure you didn't tell her you were . . . my husband?"

"Husband?" A surprised Brenda mouthed in John's direction.

"Ex-husband," John mouthed back.

"No, Case. I didn't," Wes was saying with a blank look on his face. "Did you want me to tell her I was your husband?"

John couldn't help the laugh that escaped his lips. "I'm afraid Casey's got more husbands at the moment than she knows what to do with."

Wes Carpenter gave his head a shake. "You're losing me."

Oh, Casey thought mournfully, if only I could.

3

'Tis the season to be jolly...

"I WOULDN'T BE SURPRISED if Billy Kershaw showed up next," Casey muttered.

"Who's Billy Kershaw?" John and Brenda asked, almost in unison.

Wes, who was still trying to figure out what all the fuss was about, gave Casey a puzzled look. "Yeah, who's Billy Kershaw?"

Casey sighed. "I was engaged to him briefly in my junior year at Vassar." She mindlessly stuck the baking sheet of cheese puffs into the oven. "It's the only explanation. Husbandly ghosts of Christmas past, present and future are coming to haunt me. So, any minute now, Billy Kershaw will be ringing the doorbell... Let me see. Who else could pop in?" she babbled to herself.

John gave Wes a wink. "I think she's a little punchy. A couple too many..."

Wes frowned. "Case was never a heavy drinker. A glass of wine or two. Oh, there was that one New Year's Eve a couple of years back." Wes's brown eyes sparkled and a wicked smile curved his lips.

Brenda laughed. "You don't get it, Mr. Carpenter. John was referring to husbands, not booze."

"What's this all about too many husbands? I don't get it. Is it some kind of a joke?"

"It's not a joke, Carpenter, but it is a long story," John broke in. "I don't even know the half of it yet."

Wes had been in the newspaper business long enough to know to go straight to the source. "What's going on, Case?"

The "source" was staring straight at her ex-husband, but she hadn't heard his question. "All I asked for . . . All I wanted . . ."

"What, Case?" Wes encouraged, a concerned expression on his face. In all the time he'd known Casey he'd never seen her at a loss for words. Nor had he ever seen her look so dazed. Nothing ever ruffled Casey Croyden. Well, maybe marriage had ruffled her a little. Him, too. But ever since the divorce they'd both quickly recovered their equilibrium. Now Casey looked like one good breeze would knock her flat on her butt.

"This hasn't been Casey's day," John said with a sympathetic smile in Casey's direction. "Buck up, darling. We'll figure something out. Haven't we always?"

Wes gave John a narrow gaze. "Darling? Always?" He waved an index finger back and forth between John and Casey. "You two?" He crossed his fingers symbolically. "Married?" His voice held utter disbelief. Casey had sworn off the institution after their fiasco of a marriage. "Since when?"

"It was very sudden," Brenda piped in sardonically.

Wes looked over at Brenda, then back to John, and finally gave Casey a bemused scowl. "You two are married?" He scratched his head. "I don't get it, Casey. You told me . . ." He paused to let his mind clear. "Why, only a few weeks ago, before I took off for London, you said you weren't even dating. This sure as hell must have been sudden."

"Tonight." Brenda walked over to Wes and gave his arm a little squeeze. "In a manner of speaking."

Wes rubbed his jaw and gave Brenda a baffled look. John put a comforting arm around Casey. "Don't look so worried, darling. The Matokis don't know who Wes is."

"Stop calling me 'darling,'" she spit out between clenched teeth, the glaze finally lifting from her blue eyes.

Wes shook his head, thinking that this new relationship of Casey's wasn't likely to last too long. "She has a wicked temper," he whispered to Brenda.

"John can handle it," Brenda whispered back.

Meanwhile Casey had broken loose from John's embrace and strode over to Wes, grabbing him by the belt of his trench coat. "You have to get out of here. Hurry up." She motioned to the kitchen door. "This way. I'll tell the Matokis you...you dropped in to...to make a phone call."

Wes—six-foot-two and solidly built—didn't budge. "I can't do that, darlin.'"

"Don't you call me 'darling,' either," Casey snapped. "And what do you mean, you can't do that? Of course you can do that. You just open the back door, step outside, turn right, turn right again, get into your car and go...."

"That's the part where the no can do comes in, dar...Case."

"Wes, I really don't have time to argue with you."

Wes shrugged. "I think we've got all the time in the world. Or haven't you noticed there's a raging blizzard going on outside? Driving is impossible."

"You drove up here, didn't you?"

"I barely made it. Actually I was the last car the state police let across the Dorset Bridge. You know how slippery that bridge gets in a storm. Remember last winter...."

"But...but that's the only way to the highway," Casey said, a frantic note in her voice. "That's the only way into town. That's..."

"That's too bad," Brenda offered with a solicitous smile.

"What's so bad about it?" Wes asked Casey. "It isn't as though you were planning to be alone on your honeymoon." He gave Brenda a nod and then pointed his thumb at the kitchen door. "You've got a houseful of new friends. I caught a look at two guys in the living room, the Japanese woman who met me at the door." He squinted. "Who are all these folks, Case? And what's the harm of one more? It's kind of homey what with Christmas just around the corner."

Brenda extended a hand to Wes, a bright smile on her toffee-colored lips. "I'm Brenda, one of Casey's oldest and dearest friends."

Wes blinked several times. "You are? How come we never met?"

"Oh, Wes, be quiet. I've got to think," Casey said, starting to pace. "Okay, okay, so driving is out." She took a few more steps, stopped and swirled in Wes's direction. "I know. You can stay at John and Brenda's place next door."

"John and Brenda's place?" Wes echoed.

"There's no heat or hot water there, Casey," John reminded her.

"John and Brenda's place?" Wes repeated, his tone more quizzical. He gazed at Brenda, who was still at his side. "You and John were...?"

Brenda crossed two fingers and winked at Wes. "Of course, that was before . . ." She motioned over to John and Casey.

"Ohhh . . . I see. So you two were . . ."

"Once upon a time."

Wes observed the attractive brunette with growing fascination. "And you don't mind . . . ?"

Brenda arched her brow. "Do you?"

Wes grinned. "All I want is to see Casey happy."

"My sentiments exactly . . . about John."

While Brenda and Wes were exchanging felicitous wishes for their exes, John and Casey were discussing the pros and cons of depositing Wes next door.

"He'll freeze to death over there," John pointed out.

"There's a fireplace."

"You know it doesn't work and besides, I tried it. Within five minutes the whole room was filled with smoke. The chimney probably hasn't been cleaned in fifty years."

"Wait. I have a little electric heater upstairs. We can—"

"No electricity, remember?"

"No electricity."

"The storm will probably be over by morning. They'll clear the roads and Wes can be on his merry way. What's the harm in letting him stay here overnight?"

"What's the harm? What's the harm?" Casey grabbed John's shirt. "How many men running around this house calling me 'darling' can I handle before I go stark raving mad?"

John put his hands lightly on Casey's shoulders. "We'll manage. I'll help you," he said softly.

"It's impossible."

He tilted her chin. "I had the feeling you were the kind of gal who'd never admit defeat."

Casey's eyes flew up to his face. She was very aware of the touch of his hand on her chin. That one small point of warm contact somehow managed to spread waves of heat through her whole body. "I . . . am . . . that kind of gal," she found herself saying. Here she was, in the midst of the worst catastrophe of her career, trembling with ardor like a schoolgirl, her pulse fluttering in her throat.

John smiled gently down at her.

Wes caught the tender scene between them from the corner of his eye. "There, see. That's more like it. So, what's the big problem anyway, Case?"

Casey's momentary lapse into optimism fell instantly by the wayside. She pressed her palms to her temples. "He wants to know what the problem is." A little laugh escaped her lips. It had a tinge of hysteria in it. Not a good sign. "Don't you get it, Wes? Don't you . . . see the problem?"

Wes shrugged. "Look, Casey, if you're worried that I'm jealous or that I want to horn in on you two—" He gave John a quick smile "—don't even think about it. I'm happy for you. Really I am. I just hope, this time round, you don't . . ."

Casey did a double take. "I don't what?" She folded her arms defiantly across her chest. "Are you implying, Wes Carpenter, that I was the one responsible for our marriage falling apart? That it was me . . . ? Me?"

John's arm went back around Casey. "Take it easy, darling. It's never only one person's fault. It takes two to tango as they say. Isn't that true, Brenda?"

Brenda shot John a rueful look. "One of the two does have to take the lead in the dance—darling."

John extended a hand palm up. "Yes, but if the other decides to follow the lead . . . As my mother used to say, if someone asked you to follow him off the Brooklyn Bridge. . ."

"Hey there, John," Wes broke in, "If one's strong enough, he can shove one over the bridge against one's will—if you know what I mean. And besides, these days it isn't necessarily the guy that always leads in the dance." His eyes moved to Casey.

She almost went for the bait, but then pulled herself up short. "We're all crazy. Crazy. How can we all be talking about marriage at a time like this? I've got too many husbands on my hands and we're talking about who caused who's divorce."

Wes, John and Brenda all smiled. After all, the topics were related. Casey's sense of humor, however, was temporarily out of service. She was pacing again. "I don't believe this. I just don't believe this is happening to me."

The others all spoke at once. Then the kitchen door swung open, a head popped in, and all three went instantly mute.

"Excuse me, but I think your guests are growing restless," David Quinn announced, opening the door farther. "I could use some help out there."

Wes's questioning eyes dropped to Brenda.

"Brother," Brenda mouthed.

"Brother?" Wes repeated loudly. "Casey doesn't have a brother."

David shrugged. "Yeah, I was supposed to be her husband, but that guy—" he pointed to John "—beat me to it."

Wes's expression was one of baffled admiration for his ex-wife. "My, my, darlin', you *have* been a busy queen bee while I've been gone."

John and Brenda smiled, but Casey's mouth was set in a tight, determined line. She grabbed the cheese puffs out of the oven and hastily arranged them on a serving tray. "Here—" she shoved the tray into David's chest "—just keep the Matokis occupied for a few more minutes. I'll be right out. Or I'll have gone ahead with my plan to commit hari-kari. Right now, hari-kari seems preferable."

"But I—" David started to protest.

"Don't argue with her, Quinn. I mean—Croyden," John corrected, giving Casey a wink. "We just have to think of this as a theatrical production. We have our parts to play, parts we've all had some experience with in the past." He smiled at Casey. "Buck up, darling. We'll give the performances of a lifetime. We'll bring down the house."

Casey sighed wearily. "And every last bit of it is going to fall right on top of me."

"Not a chance," John said softly. "I won't let that happen."

David was still wedging the swinging kitchen door open with his shoulder, his hands holding the tray of hors d'oeurvres. "I don't think I ever did play the role of a brother. Well, no, that's not true. I was once Uncle Vanya in an off-off-off-Broadway production. So if I was an uncle, I had to be somebody's brother...."

Casey's eyes darkened.

"Go, David," John warned him after a quick glance at Casey. One more moment and she really might pick up a butcher knife. And not to commit hari-kari, but murder!

"Okay, okay, I'll do my best. But I'm not great with the Chinese."

"Japanese," Brenda corrected the actor as he was making his exit.

Casey watched the door swing closed and then she stared at it for several moments. Three pairs of eyes watched her watching the door. Then John, Brenda and Wes started talking at the same time.

"What if . . . ?"

"I think we . . ."

"Couldn't . . . ?"

But Casey silenced them all with an assured, "I've got it."

John grinned at Wes and Brenda. "By George, she's got it. I think she's got it."

Casey's hand cupped her chin as she studied Wes thoughtfully. Then her gaze shifted to Brenda.

Brenda's right brow slowly raised as she returned Casey's stare. "Are you thinking what I think you're thinking?"

Wes looked at John. "What's she thinking?"

"You've known her longer than I have. I should be asking you."

"Casey's never been an easy woman to figure out."

"I think I've figured that much out on my own."

Wes grinned. "Then you're doing better than average."

"Will you two be quiet," Casey ordered.

John's eyes narrowed as he watched Casey shift her gaze back and forth between Wes and Brenda. "By George, I think I've got it now. Jolly good idea, darling."

Before Casey got the chance to test her idea out on Wes and Brenda, she saw the kitchen door start to swing open again. "Damn it, David. I told you to keep—"

Akiko Matoki's head peeked timidly from the door. "So sorry, Casey. I only thought I could help you with something."

Casey's complexion went ashen, her hand going up to her mouth in horror.

It was John who came to her rescue. "Don't mind, Casey, Akiko. She thought David was coming back in to...butt into something here between Wes and Brenda. You met Wes, didn't you?"

Akiko smiled. "Oh, yes, For a moment." She looked at Casey. "More family for the holidays?"

Casey's mouth opened, but no words came out.

"Friend," John said quickly, filling in the silence. "Well . . . Brenda's friend, really."

"Oh, I see," Akiko said, not sounding like she saw at all.

John strolled over to her. "You see, Akiko, it's like this." He could feel Casey's eyes intently on him as he spoke. "It's sort of a triangle situation." He smiled awkwardly. "You probably don't understand what I mean."

Akiko's eyes sparkled. "Oh, I think I understand, John. I have watched American soap operas. You mean, this gentleman and Casey's brother are both involved with Brenda."

"Nothing like that," Casey hurriedly broke in. "I mean, not at the same time. Not all three . . . together." Heaven only knew what Akiko might be imagining.

Akiko giggled. "Oh, I did not think . . ."

"No. No, of course you didn't. I just...I only..." Casey stared helplessly at John.

"It's very simple," John said, giving Casey a quick check before picking up the ball again. "David dated Brenda a long time ago. After they broke up Wes here started dating Brenda. They had a lovers' quarrel, Brenda came up here to cool her jets, and now Wes has shown up to try to put things right. Only, Brenda seems to have set off some sparks in David again. And Casey doesn't want David horning in because she knows Brenda really does love Wes." He gave Wes, Brenda and Casey a fast survey. "There, did I get it right?"

Casey gave her head a little shake, but she smiled. "I think that's it . . . in a nutshell."

Wes was rubbing his jaw again, trying to make sense out of John's rundown. He wasn't making progress, but he decided not to bother trying to figure it out for the time being.

Brenda, silent up to now, was giving Wes a curious look, a faint smile on her lips. Then she turned her gaze to Akiko. "Casey thinks David ought to give me and Wes some breathing space. David can be very persistent, right Casey?"

"Right. Oh, right. Absolutely right. I mean, I adore my brother, Akiko, but . . ."

Akiko's dark eyes sparkled. "But he's a bit of a ladies' man?"

"Oh, no, David hasn't made a pass at you, has he?" Casey gasped.

Akiko put her hand to her mouth as she laughed. "Oh, no."

Casey let out a grateful sigh.

Brenda, working hard to keep a straight face, took Wes's arm. "Come on, sweetheart. Let's find a quiet spot to talk. It was silly of me to run off the way I did. But I do feel you ought to apologize."

"Apologize?" Wes's head was beginning to swim.

Brenda gave Akiko a weary smile. "Are Japanese men as impossible as American men, Akiko?"

Akiko's dark eyes shimmered. "Some things are universal, Brenda." The two woman smiled at each other, and then Akiko stepped aside as Brenda ushered Wes from the room. After the door swung closed, Akiko once again extended an offer to help Casey with dinner.

John was the one to tell her it wasn't necessary. "We've got everything under control now. Dinner in twenty minutes. Perhaps you could keep David engaged so that Wes and Brenda . . ."

"Oh, yes, of course."

After Akiko left, John tapped his thumb against his lips. "I think Akiko winked at me," he muttered.

"What?"

"Nothing."

Casey sank against the counter and closed her eyes. When she opened them again a few moments later, John was standing in front of her.

She smiled weakly. "You were wonderful."

"You didn't do so badly yourself, darling."

"Don't—" She stopped, her smile widening. "Never mind. You've earned the right to call me anything you'd like." She tilted her head. "That was quick thinking—Wes and Brenda."

"That was your idea, wasn't it?"

Casey nodded. "More or less. Less some of the embellishments." A rueful smile curved her lips. "Did you have to include quite so many of them, though? Now we've got to figure out some way to get the rewrite to David. And he's having enough trouble playing the role of my brother. How's he going to handle a dual role, brother and jilted lover?"

"I'll get him aside and coach him."

Casey's eyes traveled John's face. Yes, he really did remind her of Clark Gable. Her heart quickened, a flush of desire swimming through her. She saw John's gaze lift to the ceiling.

"What is it?" Her voice was a breathy whisper.

His gaze lowered, his eyes fixed on hers. "No mistletoe."

Her own eyes traveled to the ceiling. "No. No, there isn't any mistletoe up there." She moistened her dry lips with her tongue.

John's eyes sparkled. "What the hell? Let's pretend."

Without quite having made up her mind to pretend, Casey found herself leaning toward him as his arms moved around her slender waist and they were kissing...for real. At first it was just the light pressure of his lips on hers. But then his tongue slid with slow deliberation across her lips, licking them. Even as her lips parted, he made no move to deepen the kiss. All in good time.

But it was Casey who was impatient, Casey whose insides were turning to liquid at John's subtle yet oh-so-erotic maneuvers, Casey who was finding herself incapable of rational thought.

He was nibbling on her lower lip, then moving to her top lip. Then his tongue was once again skimming across her mouth, tracing its contours. When it came to kissing, John was as artful and imaginative as they came. Casey's mind started wandering to more intimate possibilities.

Wait a minute, she thought, wait a minute! But just at that moment of caution, John thrust his tongue into her mouth, and Casey's brief foray into rational thought evaporated. She let out a little moan, her breath caught in her throat, and she was kissing him back, her arms tightening around his neck, her senses swimming.

He released her mouth, his lips moving to her throat. He planted tiny kisses there.

"Not fair... I can't think," Casey whispered breathlessly.

He found her mouth again, cutting off her protest, which had been weak at best. This time he kissed her softly, lingeringly, provocatively.

When John let her go, Casey opened her eyes slowly, completely disoriented. Even as she started to focus again, she couldn't meet his eyes. Instead she scooted around him and strode self-consciously to the stove.

"I've... got to make... dinner," she muttered.

John walked over to her. "I'll help." His own voice was huskier than usual.

Casey stared down at the ingredients she'd gathered for potted chicken. "I can't do this. I can't, John."

"It's only chicken, Casey. What can you do to ruin chicken?"

"No, not the chicken." Her eyes swept his face. "You. I can't go around kissing you. I can't get involved now. I've got to think about what I'm doing here."

He stood an inch from her, watching her think, which made thinking impossible. Her heart was still pounding from their kiss, and her face felt hot with excitement at the least prospect of another one. And another. And then on to...

"No," she said so fiercely John took a step back.

Casey shook some salt into the pot of chicken and turned up the burner. "If only Quinn had shown up first. Then none of this would have happened." She focused on the cookbook propped open beside the stove. "Dumplings. Why did I ever pick potted chicken with dumplings? I've never made a dumpling in my life. I don't

even like dumplings. Maybe I can do something else."
She grabbed up the heavy book.

John glanced with a smile at the name on the cover.
"*The Joy of Cooking*. Come on, darling. Surely we can
find some joy in all this."

"Very funny, John. Ho, ho, ho."

He took hold of her shoulders. "It has been kind of
funny if you think about it."

Casey was in no mood to concede. "It's not the least
bit funny. I was banking everything on making this hotel
deal with Matoki. It could mean a vice presidency for
me. Every last hotel chain in America has been beating
down Matoki's door. And I manage to get my foot in,
only to trip and fall flat on my face. And each time I get
up, I trip again."

John smiled a little smile. "I'll catch you next time."

Casey sighed. "That's just as bad. Maybe worse." She
fixed her eyes on him. "Really, Gallagher, you've got to
stop playing your part so damn well."

His smile deepened. "Do you honestly wish Quinn had
shown up first, Casey?"

"It would have been a lot less complicated if he were
my husband," Casey said in a low voice. "I'm not at all
attracted to him."

John's eyes sparkled. "What's a marriage without attraction?"

"It's the only kind I stand a chance of surviving," she
confessed. "I was lousy at my one shot at love and marriage. Wes was no better at it," she hastened to add.

John hadn't stopped smiling. "Brenda and I didn't win
any prizes, either." He cupped her chin. "But that was
Christmas past, Casey." His smiling lips started to de-
scend.

Just as his lips met hers, the swinging door flew open. "Okay, this is it," David announced. "I don't see why I have to be the total entertainment committee while the rest of you—" He stopped, eyeing the two of them narrowly. "It seems to me I've got the worst role to play here." Then he looked around. "Where's Brenda? And who was that other guy who was in here before? And why is the little Oriental woman in the living room shooting me these funny looks all of a sudden and giving me fortune cookie advice about my love life?"

John chuckled. "Just a minor alteration in the script, that's all." He walked over to David and put a friendly arm around his shoulder. "How would you like to add a little meat to your role? Have a go at something with some real substance. Passion, romance, high drama. Something you could really sink those actor teeth of yours into. What do ya say?"

David wet his lips. "Now you're talking, man. That's more like it. That's precisely what I want."

John grinned. "Well, Quinn, that's precisely what Santa's gonna bring you."

4

A partridge in a "pair" tree . . .

"THAT WAS A WONDERFUL dinner, Casey. The chicken was so tasty. And so . . . New England," Akiko said, complimenting her.

"Yes," Toho agreed. "And those dumplings were superior."

Casey smiled. "John did the dumplings." Was that a note of wifely pride in her voice? Her smile deepened at the thought.

Toho gave Brenda a shrewd look. "So you were wrong to think John was not capable in the kitchen. Your good friend's husband *is* an excellent cook."

"What do I know?" Brenda said, a tiny sparkle in her eye.

Wes, who was sitting next to Brenda, placed a hand over hers. "I'm not such a bad cook, either."

"Who are you kidding?" Casey said without thinking.

All eyes turned to her before Casey realized what she'd said. An hour without a major gaffe and she'd foolishly allowed herself to slip into a lull. "I mean . . ."

John swung an affectionate arm around Casey and gave her a little squeeze. "She means, once Wes and Brenda spent the weekend with us and Wes decided to help out with the cooking." He looked at Casey. "What was it he was attempting to make again?"

Before Casey could think up something, Brenda piped in with "Peach cobbler." She laughed. "When he took it out of the oven it looked like something a shoemaker might have concocted, not a cook. Remember that, Wes?"

Wes grinned, his hand still resting on Brenda's hand. "How could I forget, Bren?" Their eyes met and locked for a lingering moment.

Akiko and Toho smiled at the affectionate pair. Casey managed a faint smile, too. *Okay,* she thought, *you can breathe again. Everyone is handling their roles with style and grace.*

Before Casey finished that breath, however, brother, David, sitting directly across from Brenda and beside Toho Matoki, suddenly shot his arm out and grabbed Brenda's free hand.

"I can make a peach cobbler that can stand on its ear, babe. Remember that week in Jamaica. We rented that luxury condo overlooking the bay. I was really cooking then, babe. Don't you remember those candlelit meals, the sunset over the horizon, the music. We once made such beautiful music. . . ."

"David," Casey said in a low warning voice. It was just her luck the actor would turn out to be a complete ham given the right role. She gave John a sharp look. Her "husband" and his embellishments!

"Take it easy, David," Brenda said soothingly. "We all know this is a little rough on you."

Brenda managed to extricate her hand from David's, but her stunned expression at his outburst remained.

Worse was the expression on Wes's face. He actually looked as though he wanted to punch David out. And Casey had worried that her cast of players wouldn't be able to act out their parts effectively? Instead they were all getting completely carried away with their roles.

The air was charged with so much electricity, Casey expected everyone's hair to stick straight up. She looked anxiously over at Toho and Akiko. Akiko appeared fascinated by the goings-on, her eyes bright with excitement. But Toho Matoki sat rigidly in his seat, a grim and forbidding set to his features. Casey winced as Toho sternly observed her "brother."

Toho spoke. "We must learn to hold our fond memories of past pleasures within our hearts, *David-san*. That is where they can shine. Expose them to the air and they tarnish." Toho's voice was stern but not unkind.

Toho caught Casey's eye and gave her a little nod of the head. She smiled hesitantly and then hastily closed her mouth, which had dropped open while the distinguished hotel magnate was giving David his sage advice.

The dinner party sat in silence for several moments after that. The grim expression on Toho's face softened. Or at least Casey chose to see a change. There was no question that Akiko's expression was now one of pride and admiration for her husband's words of wisdom. David sat sullenly, duly admonished. Wes had removed his hand finally from Brenda's, leaving her to start gathering up the dinner plates.

"Oh, thanks, Brenda," Casey said, quickly collecting plates at her end.

Akiko joined in. Before Casey could say anything about it not being necessary for her to help, Akiko said firmly, "You must allow me to share in the chores. Otherwise I shall return home from my wonderful New England Christmas plump and lazy."

Casey observed the dainty woman's delicate frame and smiled a doubtful smile about that ever being a possibility. However, she invited Akiko to participate in the cleanup.

Akiko took a tray from the buffet and gathered up the wine goblets from the table, following Casey and Brenda into the kitchen.

"Just put everything on the counter. I'll rinse the dishes and stick them into the dishwasher later," Casey said, heading for the oven to check on the apple pie.

"Smells delicious," Brenda said.

Akiko agreed.

"Coffee or tea?" Casey asked, before pouring the coffee beans into her grinder.

"Coffee for me," Brenda said. And then she quickly added, "Oh, and for Wes."

Casey gave her head a surreptitious shake in Brenda's direction. Wes hated coffee.

Brenda's expression registered the message. "No, no, what am I thinking? Wes doesn't drink coffee anymore. He drinks . . ." She looked for a hint from Casey.

"Herbal tea?" Casey offered.

Brenda smiled brightly. "Herbal tea. His favorite. I'll make it for him."

Akiko was emptying the tray of goblets on the counter. "Toho and I will have coffee also. And what about John, Casey? Does he prefer coffee or tea?"

Casey shot a quick look at Brenda. "Coffee?" she tried to sound more thoughtful than questioning. Brenda smiled. "Coffee," Casey repeated with more assurance. Another hurdle cleared and she was still on her feet. "And I'll bring out apple pie for everyone."

"Apple pie. A perfect finish," Akiko reflected.

A perfect finish. Ah, Casey thought, wouldn't that be wonderful. She ground the beans and made the coffee while Brenda boiled water for Wes's tea and Akiko took cups and saucers off an open shelf and placed them on a serving tray. "Oh, Casey. We forgot about your brother. What does he drink? Coffee or tea?"

Right now Casey would have loved to forget about her "brother." She looked over at Brenda, who returned a little shrug.

"Does David still drink coffee, Casey?" Brenda asked.

"You know David," Casey said vaguely. "He's so . . . unpredictable."

Akiko laughed softly. "Yes, I think that's true. Men are such fascinating creatures, don't you agree? When you first arrived, Brenda, David was playing it so cool."

Casey grinned. "Playing it cool? Don't tell me they use that phrase in Japan?"

"Oh, no. But I have a daughter who went to university near Boston," Akiko explained. She waved her hand. "But that's another story. What I was observing with interest is how David's response to you changed, Brenda, after he watched you and Wes getting back together. Once he had a rival he rose to the situation. Tell me. Was Jamaica all he said it was?"

Brenda grinned. "Well, David does have a certain style. Jamaica wasn't Brooklyn. Moonlit swims, picnics on the beach. It was romantic, but his outburst just now was a bit embarrassing." Her hazel eyes sparkled. "I have to admit it was rather flattering, too."

Casey smiled to herself. Brenda didn't seem to have any complaints about her role as the femme fatale for two very attractive, assertive rivals.

Akiko observed Brenda thoughtfully. "Are you and Wes thinking about getting married, Brenda?"

Thrown by the question, Brenda hesitated. "Well, it's a little soon."

Casey was quick to agree. "Yes, I think they should get to know each other better before taking such a serious step,"

"Did you and John know each other for a long time before you got married?" Akiko asked.

Casey offered a lopsided grin as she stacked cake plates and the warm apple pie on a platter. "Long enough, Akiko. Long enough."

"Yes," Akiko said cheerfully. "You and John seem very happy together. So loving and affectionate. It's so nice to see. You hear so much about the high rate of divorce among American couples. You are most fortunate, Casey. Lasting relationships should be treasured."

Casey felt a sinking feeling in the pit of her stomach and she had difficulty meeting Akiko's eyes. "Let's not talk too much about it," she said, clearing her throat and deliberately avoiding Brenda's gaze. "Like your husband said, Akiko, we mustn't expose our treasures to the air or they might tarnish." She wiped a bead of perspiration from her brow and quickly asked Brenda to get the pitcher of milk from the fridge and the sugar bowl off the counter.

Brenda gathered up the items and gave Casey a sympathetic smile. "Are we ready?"

Casey managed a halfhearted nod.

When the three women returned to the dining room, they found John and Toho deep in an animated discussion about trade issues between Japan and the United States. Wes, who was peeling an orange he'd taken from the fruit bowl on the buffet, offered a comment or observation here or there. David sat silently, looking bored and restless. He perked up as the women returned and began serving the dessert and drinks.

Casey quickly got into the trade discussion as she dished out the apple pie. She wanted to show Toho Matoki that she was up on all the current issues to do with his country. She also was desperate to grab any opportunity to prove to Matoki that she wasn't a complete ditz!

Before she got a chance to get in more than a comment or two, Akiko changed the subject. "I was mentioning to Casey, Toho, about Hanae getting her university degree in Boston."

A shadow fell across Toho's face.

"Weren't you pleased with her education?" Casey asked him. "What university . . . ?"

"Harvard."

"Why, Harvard is one of the most prestigious universities in this country, Toho," Casey said. It also happened to be where she'd gotten her advanced degree in business, but she decided it wouldn't be wise to mention that.

Toho raised a hand to silence her. "I am well aware of the university's high standing. I was counting on that."

Akiko wagged her head. "Toho despairs because Hanae, our daughter, has returned to Tokyo with new ideas that are . . . quite exhilarating but equally exhausting."

"Exhilarating!" he said in mocking tones. "To you her ideas are exhilarating. To me they are only exhausting. And distressing. She is rude, outspoken, intent on being unconventional. . . ."

"Toho does not approve of Hanae's liberated ideas."

"Liberated?" he grumbled. "I do not call her ideas liberated. Or her behavior. Poor judgement. That's what I say."

Akiko gave the group around the table a little shake of her head. "Toho also does not approve of Hanae's boyfriend. He's a musician."

"Musician! You call that noise music?" Toho muttered.

"He's a bass player in my son's rock-and-roll band," Akiko added softly.

Toho waved his fork in frustration as he surveyed the group around the table and then let out a heavy sigh. "My son has decided he is Japan's answer to Elvis Presley. As if Japan ever sought such an answer. My boy is irresponsible, unreliable—" He stopped abruptly and surveyed Casey and John in turn, his expression almost menacing. "Are you planning to have children?"

"No," Casey said so quickly and so emphatically that John laughed.

"She's says that now, Toho, but we'll get around to it one of these days," John said, stroking Casey's cheek.

Casey went to push John's hand away, but a happily married woman in a lasting relationship probably wouldn't reject the occasional affectionate stroke. She had to grin and bear it as she said tightly, "We've got plenty of time. Right now my career is far too absorbing and so many exciting things are happening."

Wes heaved a sigh. "It's the same old story, Case."

Brenda kicked Wes in the shin. He winced but snapped to attention. "The same old story as Brenda is always giving me."

Brenda shrugged. "I don't know, Wes. One of these days I wouldn't mind settling down and having kids."

Wes gave her a curious look. "Really?"

Brenda smiled winsomely. "According to a fortune-teller who once read my cards, there are three tiny tykes in my future."

David looked up from the pie he'd been devouring. "I love kids." He gave Brenda a baleful smile. "We once talked about having kids, Brenda. We even came up with names. What was it we decided on? Zachary? No, wait. Jared. Yeah, that was it. Jared for a boy. Stephanie for a girl."

"Jared and Stephanie?" Wes countered. "Not on your life. Give me a name like Bill, Jeff, Sue . . ."

"I've always been partial to the name Ethan myself," John said, giving Casey a sly wink. "What do ya say, darling? Ethan if it's a boy?" He reached for her hand.

"John . . ." Casey said stiffly.

"How sweet, darling, wanting to name the baby after me."

He grinned provocatively and drew her hand to his lips. His lips were warm and enticing against her palm. The sensation was electrically erotic and Casey had to fortify herself with a deep breath.

Akiko's eyes sparkled. "Children are a blessing, Casey. Oh, they make you fret and they distress you at times, but they are a joy."

"Hanae was the sweetest little girl," said Toho with a smile of reminiscence. "And my son, Tomita, was smart as a whip, as they say in your country. And, best of all, both children were obedient." He sighed heavily. "If only they could stay young."

Akiko gave her husband an understanding and tender pat on the shoulder while she beamed at John and Casey. "The two of you would make beautiful children. Both of you are so very attractive."

John was still holding Casey's hand, which he'd now placed on his thigh, his thumb lightly, provocatively caressing her skin. Casey was so distracted by John's feathery strokes—even more distracted by the feel of his solid, muscular thigh beneath her palm—that she couldn't even manage a polite thank-you to Akiko for her compliment. John thanked her for them both.

Casey finally extricated her hand and offered everyone second helpings of pie and coffee.

"No more for me, darling," John said, stretching. He fought back a yawn. "Sorry. I'm a little tired. Exhausting afternoon at the lumberyard. Going over the measurements and then figuring out everything I'm going to need to construct my. . . hut."

Casey caught John's sly smile, but she answered him with one of benign innocence. "I'm sure your hut is going to come out perfectly fine," she said firmly.

Wes rubbed his hands together. "Well, I think I'll turn in early, if that's okay with everyone."

"That sounds like a good idea," Toho said, glancing at his wristwatch. "It is ten o'clock. Akiko and I are still in the throes of jet lag."

David rose. "I'm pretty tired myself. It's a long drive from—"

"Philly," Casey hastily interjected before David slipped up and said New York.

John rose, too. "Why don't you show all of our guests to their rooms, darling, and I'll clean up down here."

"Good idea," Casey said, wondering what to do about the sleeping arrangements for Wes and Brenda. Would the Matokis assume the lovers would share a bedroom? And would David then decide this called for another outburst of irate jealousy?

Brenda came to Casey's rescue by specifying a single room for the night. Brenda looked over at Wes. "I think we both need a little time and space to think things through."

"I thought you accepted my apology," Wes said.

Brenda smiled. "Let's not rush things."

"If that's really what you want, Bren," he said with just the right hint of disappointment.

Casey looked quizzically at Wes. She had the distinct impression his disappointment wasn't entirely put on. Wouldn't it be funny, she thought, if Wes and Brenda really did end up hitting it off? That thought immediately led into another one. What if she and John ended up as a pair? Now that, she decided, wasn't so funny.

"EVERYONE TUCKED IN for the night?" John stuck the last of the dishes into the dishwasher and turned around to face Casey, who had just come into the kitchen.

Casey leaned wearily against the doorjamb. "Yes, thank heavens. What a night!"

John grinned. "I can't recall one like it ever before."

"You've really saved my neck, John." Casey hesitated. "But..."

"But?" He pressed the button on the dishwasher.

"This isn't easy, John."

He folded his arms across his broad chest and studied her closely. "No, you're right. It's a damn sight harder than I bargained for."

"Are you sorry I got you into this?" she asked.

"How often does a guy get a proposal this unique?" He moved closer to her. "From such a unique woman?"

Casey held up her hand. "Don't. Let's not make this even harder. We have to sleep together tonight," she blurted out.

John's blue eyes sparkled. "This is getting more unique by the moment."

"That's not what I mean and you know it. We have to appear to be sleeping together. That is . . . we have to share a bedroom. But I have that all worked out. There's a little nursery attached to the bedroom. It's sort of an alcove, with a convertible sofa. It's perfectly comfortable. But if you'd prefer that I slept there and you took the bedroom . . ."

He didn't respond, but he did start walking toward her again.

She hurried on. "There's no reason why we can't . . . be adult about this. No reason why we can't . . . honor each other's privacy. There's no reason to . . . to . . . let things get out of hand."

He was right beside her, his warm breath ruffling her hair. "Do you want a reason, Casey?"

"John . . . please. You can't begin to know how much this deal with Matoki means to me. I've probably screwed it up already. He must think I'm a stuttering, stammering idiot."

"He thinks you're delightful."

Casey's eyes shot up in disbelief to John's face. He was smiling, but it wasn't a teasing smile. It was soft, tender, incredibly appealing. "You mean it? He . . . told you?"

"He's having a great time, Casey. And so is Akiko. He told me he'd never expected his visit would be this much fun."

"Oh, John . . ." Casey said, too relieved to finish.

"Come on, darling. Let's go to bed."

Casey gave him a wary look.

He smiled. "I'll take the alcove."

"Oh, John. You really are wonderful."

He brushed her cheek with his palm. "Maybe, before this holiday is over, you'll decide that's reason enough," he murmured.

Casey sighed. "It's not that it isn't tempting. But . . ."

He put a finger to her lips. "Let's leave it at that, Casey. I can at least have pleasant dreams."

Casey turned off the lights in the kitchen, checked the locks on the doors and took a last look at the Christmas tree in the living room. John stood beside her.

"Nice," he said softly.

"It leans a little," Casey murmured.

"The tree?"

"The whole room."

"I love Christmas."

Casey smiled. "Me, too."

He slipped his arm lightly around Casey's shoulder. "Look." He tipped her head up.

Mistletoe.

He brushed her lips lightly, took her hand, and they went upstairs.

Casey helped John unfold the convertible couch in the alcove and make it up.

"Are you sure you wouldn't rather take the bedroom?" Casey asked.

"This will be fine," John assured her.

She showed him the adjoining bathroom that they would both have to share. "Go ahead. You wash up first. I have some paper work to do before I turn in."

"So, Wes was right."

Casey gave John a puzzled look. "Right about what?"

"The same old story. Work, work, work. Is that what did your marriage in, Casey?"

"What happened to your 'it takes two to tango' theory?" she snapped.

John put his hands up in a gesture of mock guilt. "Sorry."

"And what did your marriage in, John? Who wanted the divorce? You or Brenda?"

John clearly didn't like being questioned about his failed marriage. "It was a mutual decision," he said succinctly.

"Did you break up in Japan?" she persisted.

"In Japan?"

"When you were working over there for General Lee's Fried Chicken franchise? You and Brenda were married then, weren't you? I heard her mention that she'd stayed at one of Matoki's hotels in Tokyo."

"She came out there to see me. But she didn't stay."

"Because of problems between you?"

"Partly. And she had her own work."

"What does she do?"

"She's a secretary at a law firm." John started to close the bathroom door.

"And are you still with General Lee?" Casey asked before the door closed.

"No. I'm in between jobs at the moment."

"Oh, I see." Casey hesitated. "Well, that offer still goes."

John reopened the door. "What offer is that?"

Casey felt awkward. "The money. Three hundred a day."

John grinned. "No, thanks. But I'll tell you what you can do. Put a present under the Christmas tree for me. I love opening presents on Christmas morning."

Casey laughed. "Me, too."

"Maybe Santa will have something special for you under the tree, as well," he said with a wink, and shut the door.

Casey pulled out her files and spread them on her bed. She fluffed up the pillows and stretched out, still dressed. She'd wait for John to finish with the bathroom and settle in for the night before getting into her nightgown. She picked up the closest file and opened it.

She could hear the sound of the shower through the closed bathroom door as she tried to focus on the top sheet in her file on the Hammond plan for the hotel deal with Matoki. Since John's comment that Matoki seemed unperturbed by the way his first day in "tranquil" Vermont had unfolded, Casey was filled with renewed optimism.

That wasn't all she was filled with. Her eyes strayed to the closed bathroom door, visions of her "husband" dancing in her head. She could hear John singing. "'On the twelfth day of Christmas my true love gave to me, a partridge...'"

Casey pulled her gaze away. Now if she could just pull her mind away from the fantasy of John's strong, virile body glistening with the spray of water...

"'On the eleventh day of Christmas my true love gave to me...'"

She switched on the radio beside her bed. Bing Crosby was crooning a Christmas ditty, "'I'm dreaming of a white Christmas.'" Casey got out of bed and went over to the window, drawing the white curtain. It was still snowing hard. If it kept up over night, there'd be over a foot of snow by tomorrow. And if it kept up through tomorrow, they might not be dug out for days. Casey shut her eyes. Days with her make-believe friends and make-believe brother. Days—and nights—with a make-believe husband who was wreaking havoc on her pulse rate.

The bathroom door opened and John stepped out, clad only in his trousers. Casey's pulse rate became instantly erratic as her eyes fixed on his broad, well-muscled, naked chest. The file slipped unnoticed from her hand.

"Your turn," John said with an airy wave. "Want me to wash your back?"

Wash me, rinse me, stroke me, kiss me... "No, thanks. I've gotten used to managing on my own."

"Well, good night, then." John cast a glance over at the paper-strewn bed. "Will you be up late?"

Casey grabbed a cotton flannel nightgown from her top bureau drawer and headed for the bathroom. "If you're worried about the light bothering you, we can string up a curtain across the alcove entry."

John laughed. "The walls of Jericho?"

Casey didn't get it.

"From a famous old Clark Gable movie called *It Happened One Night.*"

Casey looked back over her shoulder at John. "What happened?"

John grinned. "The walls of Jericho came tumbling down." He winked broadly and Casey firmly shut the bathroom door.

She was in bed under the covers ten minutes later. Not a sound from the alcove. She hoped John was the kind of man who fell asleep as soon as his head hit the pillow. Wes was like that. Probably from traveling so much. He'd learned to grab sleep quickly and easily whenever he had the chance.

Casey switched off the overhead light and turned on the lamp beside her bed, picked up the file she'd gotten nowhere with before and forced herself to concentrate.

She hadn't made it through the first page, when she heard a knock on her door. She looked up with alarm. "Yes?"

"Excuse me, Casey. I saw the light on under your door..."

"Akiko?"

"I have a little something for you. For you and John. I forgot all about it earlier. May I give it to you now? It's something you might enjoy having in the morning."

"Oh ... okay. Just ... a minute, Akiko." Casey threw off the covers, leaped out of bed and dashed into the alcove.

"John," she whispered, shaking him. Her luck. He had fallen asleep instantly.

"John, wake up. Akiko wants to give us something."

"Hmmmm?"

"John, please, you've got to get into my bed. If I open the door and she doesn't see you there, she'll get suspicious."

John tried to pull the cover over his head. "Tell her we're sleeping."

"She already knows I'm awake. She saw the light shining under the door. John, please. Just for a minute." Without waiting for his consent she grabbed at the covers and started tugging them off him.

"Okay, okay," John muttered groggily. "Just let me..." He went to reach for his trousers on the floor.

"There's no time for dressing. Hurry into my bed," Casey pleaded as she rushed out of the alcove. "Coming, Akiko." She grabbed her robe, threw it on and got to the door.

"Hold on a sec," John called to her in a low whisper. "I'm not in bed yet."

Casey turned around impatiently, her hand on the doorknob. "Well, hurry—" Casey swallowed the rest of the sentence, her eyes widening. Climbing into her bed, John had let the sheet he'd wrapped around him drop to the carpet. "Oh, my goodness," she gasped, "you're . . . naked."

John gave Casey a raunchy wink, slid under her covers and put his finger to his lips. "Shhh, darling. Let's keep it in the family."

5

All is calm, all is bright . . .

"I HOPE I DID NOT disturb you, Casey," Akiko said apologetically as she stood, wrapped in a teal-blue kimono, at Casey's open bedroom door.

"Oh . . . no. Of course not. We were . . . up. Right, darling?" Casey cast a quick glance over her shoulder in John's general direction, but she couldn't quite bring herself to meet the eye of the naked man tucked in her bed.

"Not at all, Akiko," John said amiably, sounding fully awake now. "Casey was going through some files, and I was just relaxing, waiting for her to finish up so we could turn in for the night."

Akiko extended two neatly wrapped packages she was holding in her hands. "I meant to give these to you, Casey, when we arrived, but then there were so many . . ."

"Distractions?" Casey sighed. "Believe me, Akiko, it wasn't what I'd planned for your first day here."

"Our first day was to be tomorrow. We are so sorry, Toho and I, to have caused you inconvenience."

"Inconvenience? Oh, you mean the business with the bathtub when you first arrived?" Casey gave a little wave of her hand. "It was only water," she said airily.

"I hope you are not suffering any pain from your fall."

"Oh, no. No. Not a twinge. I'm fine." Casey hesitated. "But your husband . . . is he all right? I was mortified when I landed on top of him."

"Wait a sec," John interrupted from the bed. "You fell in the bathtub, Casey? On top of Toho?"

Akiko giggled. "Oh, no. Not in the bathtub. Down the stairs."

"Casey fell down the stairs?"

"Yes. And Toho tried to break her fall. I believe," Akiko said thoughtfully, "it was the fault of the bubble bath."

John gave the two women a bewildered look. And he'd thought all the action had begun after his arrival on the scene! "The bubble bath? In the bathtub?"

"The problem was the bubble bath on the stairs," Akiko explained, hoping that would clarify the matter.

It only served to perplex John further. As he started to ask another question, Casey quickly cut him off.

"I'll fill you in later, John," she said tersely.

Akiko looked alarmed. "Oh, I am so sorry, Casey. I did not mean to say anything that you meant to keep private."

"Oh, no, it's nothing like that," Casey said hurriedly. "I just haven't gotten around to filling John in yet. What with so many people arriving and there being so much to do. But John and I never keep secrets from each other. Do we, darling?"

"No," John confirmed with less assurance than Casey would have liked.

"Anyway," Casey jumped in, "It wasn't exactly a quiet, relaxed day for you and Toho."

"Do not be at all concerned about that, Casey. Toho and I have had a most delightful first day. We look forward to equally delightful days to come."

Casey smiled weakly. If she had another "delightful" day to equal this one, someone would have to phone for the men in white jackets to come cart her off.

"Leave it to Casey, Akiko. She's full of surprises, this wife of mine."

Casey cast John a taciturn look, but he merely smiled back . . . a provocative smile at that.

"Aren't you going to open up the gifts Akiko's brought us, darling?"

Casey looked down at the packages. "Oh, I thought I'd put these under the tree, open them Christmas Day," Casey said, anxious to get rid of Akiko and call an end to this exhausting and ever more humiliating charade . . . at least for the night.

"Oh, no," Akiko said firmly. "These are not Christmas gifts, Casey. Please open them now. They're what you Americans call house gifts, I believe."

"Housewarming gifts," John offered, as he fluffed up the pillows behind him, tucked the covers halfway up his naked chest and folded his arms casually behind his head. "Come in, come in, Akiko. There's a draft from the door."

Casey tossed a gaze back at John that could have melted granite. "If you're feeling chilled, darling, why not put something—more—on?"

"That's a thought," he said cheerily, starting to lift the covers off him.

"No, no. I'll bring you something," Casey said hastily.

"Oh, no." Akiko was now in the room and closing the door. "That won't be necessary."

Casey and John both gave Akiko a classic double take. They both knew the Japanese had very different attitudes and philosophy about nudity but . . .

Akiko giggled softly. "I only mean that you will not need any further covering after you open the packages." She smoothed back a strand of glossy black hair from her delicate face.

Casey opened the first package and pulled out an intricately patterned blue-and-white soft cotton robe with a matching tie.

"A real *yukata*," John said enthusiastically from bed. "Wonderful. A touch of Japan in New England. A very thoughtful gift, Akiko."

Akiko beamed. "Yes, that's right, John. A *yukata*— what you call a robe in this country."

"I loved the one I bought in Japan. Wore it all the time. What ever became of that *yukata*, Casey?"

Casey was having a hard time containing her temper at John's warped sense of humor, but her voice was syrupy sweet as she replied, "I really don't know, darling. Perhaps you never brought it back with you from Japan."

John's grin was pointedly lecherous. "Of course I brought it back, darling. Don't you remember how you wore it on our honeymoon? Why, you said it was the softest thing against your skin next to ..."

"Really, darling," Casey said sharply. "This isn't exactly the time or place ... You're embarrassing ... Akiko."

But it wasn't Akiko's creamy white cheeks that bore the rosy hue.

John smiled contritely. "Sorry, Akiko. I guess I got carried away seeing the *yukata*, remembering ..."

"John," Casey warned sharply.

Akiko laughed softly. "Your husband is a tease, Casey. Like Toho. You wouldn't guess to look at him, but Toho takes great pleasure in such games. I pretend to get angry with him, but really I would be most distressed if he were to tire of the game. It is a sign of his affection. Of his love for me." Akiko gave Casey's shoulder a gentle pat. "Just as it is a sign of John's love for you, yes?"

Casey had to really work hard at her smile. "That's one way to look at it."

Akiko nodded and looked down at the *yukata* that Casey was holding. "This *yukata* is for you. In the other package is a matching one in a large size. For you, John." She gave him a sly smile. "I hope you will have equally fond memories of this *yukata* in years to come."

John gave Casey a brief searing glance, his dark eyes sparkling. "Something tells me I just might, Akiko. I just might at that."

"I'm so pleased. Now I shall say good night and wish you very pleasant dreams," Akiko said, bowing slightly and heading for the door.

Casey felt a flash of alarm at being left alone with the naked man in her bed. She escorted Akiko to the door. "Can I do anything for you before we all turn in? A cup of tea? I'll have one with you. We can go downstairs together."

"Oh, no, thank you, Casey. Toho is expecting me back. He never sleeps well until I am beside him."

"I know just how he feels," John confirmed, giving the empty side of Casey's double bed a little pat. "I feel the same way."

Casey glared at him and then hurried to follow Akiko, who was halfway out the door. She nearly tripped over the delicate woman's tiny heels. "Extra blankets? I could bring you extra blankets."

Akiko turned and patted Casey's hand gently. "You stay here with your husband. Before you go to bed, perhaps you and John may enjoy modeling your new *yukata*s for each other." She gave her hostess a devilish little wink and departed.

Casey turned slowly to face John. He was still nestled comfortably under her covers. Then, without a word, she closed the door and tossed John the remaining package.

"Talk about the perfect gift," Casey said sardonically as he unwrapped his *yukata*. "You might have warned me you slept in the raw when I asked you to get out of your bed before."

John slipped on the *yukata*, but made no effort to rise. "I did make a grab for my trousers, but you were so eager to get me into your bed . . ."

"Very funny. I just assumed you were wearing something."

"I always sleep in the raw, but even if I had wanted to sleep in more than my boxer shorts it would have been difficult. All my clothes are still next door."

Casey frowned. "Oh, right. Brenda's got the same problem. I had to lend her a nightgown and robe. I forgot about that."

"We'll work it out in the morning," John said, stretching and yawning at the same time.

"Morning," Casey muttered glumly as she walked over to the window. "It's still snowing out. If it keeps up through tomorrow . . ."

"We'll all gather round the piano, sing Christmas carols, bob for apples. Does brother David play the piano, darling?"

"You're really enjoying all this, aren't you?" She began mimicking John. "Whatever happened to my *yukata*, darling? And Remember our honeymoon? Remember how soft the robe felt against your skin? Almost as soft as...? Really, John. You are a tease. A terrible tease."

"Akiko says it's a sign of love and affection."

"Is that what it is? So tell me, did you tease Brenda when the two of you were married?"

"No, not very often. I suppose no one's ever brought out the tease in me quite like you, Casey." His eyes met hers and held them.

Casey shook her head in wonder. "This has been the craziest day," she said, unable to unlock her gaze from John's.

"And a crazy night," John said softly, seductively... temptingly.

Casey closed her eyes. "Too crazy for me. Please go to bed."

"I am in bed."

She opened her eyes. "Don't do this to me, John. I've already made enough mistakes for one day. If Santa's out there making his list of who's been naughty..."

John laughed. "Don't tell me you still believe in Santa Claus, Casey," he said gently, rising from her bed and fitting his *yukata* around his broad, muscular, naked frame.

"Don't tease me any more." She could feel her heart start to pound as he moved toward her. She gave him an urgent, helpless gaze. He kept on. There was a smoldering look in his dark eyes. Clark Gable eyes. Sexy, haunting, defiant... incredibly alluring.

Casey's fingers trembled as she clutched her flannel robe across her chest. "Don't come any closer, John. The game is over for the night. It isn't funny. Nothing about this whole miserable day has been the least bit funny."

He was beside her. He leaned toward her, his lips touching hers for a breath of a kiss. "Oh, come on, Casey. Some of it was pretty funny."

The contact had the most startling effect on Casey, her anxiety and wariness mixing with a strange, heady excitement.

John's dangerous dark eyes fixed on her face. He was smiling tenderly. "How about David's outburst at the dinner table? That deserves a chuckle or two." He captured David's expression perfectly and began an expert mimicking of the actor's high-timbred voice. "Remember Jamaica, babe. We made beautiful music in Jamaica, didn't we?"

A tremulous smile slowly curved Casey's lips.

John continued the imitation. "What was it we were going to name our little tykes, babe? Stephanie for a girl?"

Casey laughed. "And Jared for a boy." Her mimicking of David wasn't bad, either.

"And then there was Wes piping up with—" John quickly took on Wes's laid-back persona and voice— "give me a good solid name like Bill, Jeff, Sue."

Casey began giggling.

John joined in, his hands finding their way to Casey's shoulders as they both laughed heartily. Catching her breath, Casey proceeded to fill John in on the details of the cascading bubble bath episode followed by her ignominious tumble down the stairs and her collision with Toho Matoki. John began laughing so much tears started rolling down his cheeks.

"Stop laughing," Casey said between her own peals of laughter. "It wasn't funny at the time. I thought it was all over. My big chance with Matoki and I nearly crush him to death."

They were both laughing so hard now they were
holding on to each other. The day's tension expended it-
self in several minutes of uncontrolled hilarity. With sides
aching they collapsed against each other, fighting for
breath. But even after a minute or two, after the laughter had completely ceased, Casey still found herself
breathless. Only now it had nothing to do with having
laughed so long. It had to do with the moist heat of John's
breath against her hair, the potent effect of his hard body
pressing into her, his thin *yukata* in no way masking the
equally potent effect she was having on him.

John eased her back gently. His eyes never leaving her
face, he moved his hands to the tie of her flannel robe and
he began unfastening the knot.

"What . . . are you doing?" Casey's voice was a mere
whisper.

"Following Akiko's suggestion. That we model our
*yukata*s for each other." He slid her robe off her shoulders, revealing a modest creamy cotton flannel nightgown, one that Casey had chosen deliberately to wear,
knowing she'd be sharing the bedroom with a new "husband." Under normal circumstances, she, too, preferred
to sleep in the nude, even in winter. She loved the feel of
her warm down comforter against her chilled skin.

Casey felt exposed under John's probing gaze despite
her neck-to-toe covering. "My... *yukata* is...over there."
She pointed an unsteady finger across the room where
she'd slung her gift over a chair.

John held her fast as she started to move. "All in good
time, Casey."

"Don't do this to me, John. We don't even know each
other." She raised her blue eyes to his face in confusion
and desire. "This isn't right," she said plaintively.

He gave her a teasing smile. "But we're married. Doesn't that make it right?"

"Don't tease me now. I'm feeling too . . . susceptible." She couldn't tear her gaze away from the heated passion emanating from his dark brown eyes, but she did wrap her arms protectively across her breasts, alarmed to feel the protruding hardness of her nipples against the fine spun cotton gown.

Slowly John's hands drew her arms away from her breasts. Then, with sensuous deliberation, his palms moved over her breasts in light, caressing strokes. The thin cloth seemed to melt away beneath the heat of his hands. Casey could feel herself sinking into a state of pure, hopeless longing, Nothing but John's tender, provocative seduction seemed to matter at the moment. Not the Matokis down the hall. Not her ex-husband or John's ex-wife only a few doors down. Not the fact that she knew almost nothing about John Gallagher. Except that he could put Gable to shame, that he was an irrepressible tease, that he was the most enticing, incredibly appealing man who'd ever shown up on her doorstep.

"Oh, John," she whispered with a mixture of alarm and longing. "If only you had been more like Danny DeVito none of this would be happening to me."

"Danny DeVito?"

"Never mind."

John's smile was tantalizing. "Nothing in my entire life has quite prepared me for someone like you, Casey Croyden." One hand traveled up from her breast to her throat, his thumb caressing the hollow center where her pulse raced.

Casey's head tilted up. Her lips parted. Her resistance hung by the thinnest thread. John had only to touch it and it would break.

As his lips descended, Casey could feel her resistance snap, the urgency suffusing every pore of her body. His kiss deepened, his hands moving down her back, over her buttocks. She could feel the chill night air against her flesh as he slowly gathered the cloth of her gown in his hands and edged it up over her body. She helped him pull it over her head and fling it to the carpet. Resistance gone, Casey was left with nothing but a burning intense need for John that now completely absorbed her.

John drew her back, his eyes traveling down her naked body. He was held spellbound. He thought her body flawless, perfect. Just looking at her excited him to a fever pitch.

"Oh, John, John . . . this is crazy."

He shook his head slowly, his gaze like a warm caress over her body. "No, Casey. It isn't crazy. It's the sanest thing we could do."

"But . . . I don't even know who you are. I don't know anything about you. This is all based on some insane mistake . . ."

John's smile was mixed with tenderness, amusement and arousal. "Haven't you ever heard of miracles, Casey? Miracles are supposed to happen this time of year."

He kissed her, softly at first, but urged on by Casey, he deepened the kiss, his tongue thrusting past her teeth and inside the warm recesses of her mouth.

Casey's hands slid between their bodies, slipping inside the folds of his *yukata*, stroking and caressing his broad naked chest. Then she sought the tie of his robe, undid it and started to tug the robe off his shoulders.

Just as the *yukata* was nearly off, John stopped her, pulling her from him so abruptly that Casey felt a heart-wrenching jolt.

"Wait," John said sharply.

Wait? What was he saying? Casey's head was spinning. Wait—I've changed my mind? Wait—you're rushing it? Casey was brought up short by his command, reason rushing back in with a vengeance.

What was she doing, anyway? Undressing a perfect stranger—that's what she was doing. Succumbing to passion when she should be marshaling her precious time for planning to regain the confidence of Toho Matoki, who had to think by now that she was a total screwball. This romantic interlude was a big mistake. A big mistake. John and his miracles! She was going to need a miracle to happen, all right, if she was going to survive Christmas, never mind nail down the Matoki deal.

John's hushed tones weren't getting through to Casey. Finally he gave her a little shake. "Casey, the door," he said more sharply, pulling his *yukata* back over his naked body and knotting the tie. "There's someone knocking at your door."

It took a few moments for John's message to register. And then she heard the knock herself. Her eyes shot up with alarm to John's face. "Not Akiko again?"

John smiled seductively as he lowered his gaze to her naked body. "Maybe she wants to see how we look in our *yukata*s."

Casey's cheeks reddened and she made a mad dash across the room for her *yukata*. She was giving the knot of her tie belt a firm tug when a feminine voice wafted through the closed door.

"Casey? Are you up?"

It wasn't Akiko.

John frowned. "What does Brenda want?"

"She's your wife. You tell me."

"Ex-wife," John corrected.

"Casey." Brenda's voice was louder. "I need to talk to you."

Casey became alarmed. "You don't think she's changed her mind about . . . everything, do you?"

"Not Brenda," John said reassuringly, walking over to Casey, giving her a light kiss on the forehead and then going to the door.

"Oh," Brenda said as John opened the door. "So you're up, too."

John made a sweeping motion with his hand. "Come on in, Brenda."

"Yes," Casey piped up, distressed by the breathiness in her voice. "Yes, come in, Brenda. John and I are both up. We were just talking . . . about this and that."

Brenda stepped inside, looked over at Casey and then back at John. "Twin Japanese bathrobes. How cute." She gave Casey a sly smile. "You have thought of everything."

Casey's hand went to her chest. "Oh, no. It wasn't my idea. I didn't . . ."

"Housewarming gifts for the host and hostess from Akiko Matoki," John said, casually adjusting his *yukata* so it closed more fully.

Casey couldn't help but marvel at John's calm, collected manner. And she couldn't help but cringe at catching Brenda eyeing John's readjustment of his robe.

But Brenda's expression was merely one of wry amusement. "Looks good. On both of you," she said blithely.

Casey's hand was clutching her *yukata* closed. "Akiko just left. A minute ago. Less than a minute ago. I'm surprised you didn't collide in the hallway."

"No, we didn't." Brenda's gaze had shifted across the room. Casey followed her gaze and blanched. There was her robe and nightgown in a discarded heap on the floor.

A low unbidden moan of embarrassment escaped from Casey's throat.

"It isn't . . . what it seems," she started to explain. "We were just . . ." She shrugged helplessly. "Modeling our *yukata*s for each other. Weren't we, John?"

Before John could respond—and heaven only knew what his response would be—Brenda broke in.

"Relax, Casey. You didn't cast me in the role of irate wife now, did you?"

"I just don't want you to think . . ."

"To be perfectly frank, Casey, I'm too busy at the moment thinking about Wes Carpenter to have any thoughts to spare about you and John."

"There's nothing for you to think about concerning me and John." And then after the skip of a beat she added, "Wes?"

"Is it really over between you and Wes?" Brenda asked directly. "He says it is, but I want to know where you stand. You haven't been divorced all that long. You could still be feeling something for him. The thing is, I find him very attractive." She smiled at John. "In a different way than you, of course. You don't mind, do you?"

John put an affectionate arm around Brenda. "So that's how it is, is it?"

Brenda laughed. "Crazy, isn't it?"

"Oh, I don't know," John drawled.

Casey stared in astonishment at the divorced pair. "Of course it's crazy. We're all crazy. And there isn't even a full moon out tonight," she muttered.

"I'm not saying it could actually lead to anything," Brenda blithely went on. "But there were these definite

sparks going off between us. I think you must have noticed."

"There were supposed to be sparks," Casey said defensively, not wanting to admit Brenda was right.
Somehow Casey felt that if she could exercise some control over Brenda and Wes getting carried away with the
charade, maybe she'd stand a chance of gaining ground
over her own runaway feelings. "You're supposed to be
attracted to each other. You're just letting yourselves get
too caught up in your roles. You two don't know each
other from Adam. For goodness sake, Brenda get a grip
on yourself."

Brenda gave Casey a funny look. "Well, maybe we are
getting a bit carried away with the fun."

"Fun? Fun?" Casey's voice went up two octaves. "This
isn't fun. This is lunacy."

John started toward her, a calming smile on his face.

But Casey leaped back. "No. Stay away from me. I
mean that, John. You'd just better get a grip on yourself,
too," she shouted at him.

John came to an abrupt halt. But not because of
Casey's sharp warning. All three of the occupants of the
bedroom froze in place as a new voice wafted through
Casey's closed door.

"Case? I gotta talk to you."

Casey could only stare at John and Brenda.

"Case? Is Brenda in there with you? She's not in her
room."

It was Brenda who opened the door.

Wes beamed. "Oh, hi. I stopped by your room. I
thought we could talk for a while. I was having trouble
sleeping." He gave a half nod to John and Casey, then
looked again at the pair and grinned. "Hey, neat matching outfits. We never did that, Case."

Casey was beyond feeling anything but numb. "No, Wes, we never did."

Wes gave an amiable shrug. "Not my thing anyway."

John laughed. "To each his own, I guess."

Wes's eyes were fixed on Brenda. "Yea, my sentiments exactly." He smiled tantalizingly at her as he leaned against the doorjamb. "So, Bren, you want to talk for a while?"

Before Brenda had a chance to answer, a door opened across the hall and a pajama-clad figure stepped out of his room. "Hey, why didn't anyone tell me there was a late-night party going on?" David said petulantly as he peered over Wes's shoulder at Casey's open door. He brushed past Wes and walked into the room. "Or is this a rehearsal?" he asked Casey in hushed tones. "I could use a rehearsal myself. I'm really beginning to get into my character, seeing all the dimensions of his personality. Brother, lover, rival. The way I see it—" he glanced around at the others "—my character plays a pivotal role in the drama."

"Drama?" Casey muttered desolately. "Farce is more like it."

David didn't hear her. "What's significant here is that I see my character as a catalyst, the one who provokes a crucial change in each one of you. Your characters are forced to respond. You must feel the intensity of emotions building, respond to those feelings. Not hold anything back."

David gave his costars a rueful frown. "I gotta tell you, speaking as the only real professional here, that you're all having problems. You all have this tendency to slip in and out of your roles too much. Take you, Casey. John's your husband, right? Now you've got to believe that

fully. I kept picking up a resistance on your part. Now as
Stanislavski said . . ."

Casey started to laugh. As soon as John's eye caught
hers, he joined in. Then Brenda and Wes began laughing. Poor David looked completely befuddled.

"I don't get it. I don't get the joke."

As it turned out, David wasn't the only one who didn't
get the joke.

Toho Matoki was awakened by the raucous laughter
coming from down the hall. He nudged his wife lying
beside him. "What is that all about?"

"It must be a traditional New England custom," Akiko
replied with a little chuckle. Then she rolled over to face
her husband, snuggled her hips sensually against his and
gave him a most amorous kiss on his mouth.

6

Sleep in heavenly peace...

CASEY'S CLOCK RADIO woke her at 9:00 a.m. to the strains of "Silent Night." Eyes closed, she fished around for the snooze alarm and slammed it down just as Bing was crooning "'All is calm, all is bright...'"

John, freshly showered and wrapped in his *yukata*, stepped out from the alcove, where he'd ended up spending the night. And where Casey had firmly told him she intended him to spend all the remaining nights of his stay.

"Good morning," he said cheerily.

Casey opened one eye. "Is it still snowing?"

He walked over to the window, drew back the curtain and looked out. "Yup."

Casey grunted, rolled over on her stomach and pulled the covers up over her head. "Then there's nothing good about it."

A moment later, she felt the weight of her bed shift as John sat down beside her.

"Go away."

John tugged the covers down a couple of inches. "What can I do to put you in the holiday spirit, darling?"

She turned her head to the side and gave him a narrow one-eyed look. "Give me back yesterday. Let me start it all over again."

"How can you be sure it will go any better?"

"One thing you should know about me, I never make the same mistakes twice," she said pointedly.

John got the message and smiled. "Well, that alone should make today better. Especially after all those great pointers our actor in residence gave us last night."

Casey started to giggle but deliberately cut it off short. "Don't make me laugh. I'm miserable. I dread facing the day. All I can think about is, what can go wrong next? When is this whole pathetic charade going to come tumbling down on top of me?"

"Hey, what kind of pessimistic talk is that from a hotshot career woman like you, Croyden?"

Casey gave him a baleful look. "I know you're teasing me, but I really am a hotshot. This is not the real me. Before yesterday I was a sharp, decisive, unflappable businesswoman. In six short years I've risen from a junior exec to head of Hammond's acquisition department. That was no easy feat."

John grinned. "I'd say you have great feet, darling. Great feet, great . . ."

"What am I going to do about this mess?"

"Cheer up, darling. Matoki's a pushover. You'll do fine with him."

"It's me and you I'm worried about." Her smile was withering. "You probably find this hard to believe, but I . . . I don't rattle easily. I really don't."

He gently smoothed her hair back from her cheek. "I believe you," he said softly.

"You do?"

"I do."

Casey looked up at him. "You could get in trouble saying 'I do' so lightly," she said in a weak attempt at humor.

John obliged her with a laugh, but his expression quickly turned serious. "I have no regrets, Casey."

She rolled over on her back and edged the covers down below her chin. "I guess we both got a little carried away last night."

"And Quinn accused us of not getting into our characters strongly enough."

Casey's gaze flicked over John's ruggedly handsome face. He really did remind her of Clark Gable. Gable in his prime, with eyes glowing like bedside lamps, a mouth radiating virility and humor. A smile tugged at the corners of Casey's mouth. "I haven't played a role with that kind of enthusiasm for a long time."

John gave her a Gable grin. "Neither have I."

"But we've really got to—"

"Get a grip on ourselves?"

Casey nodded. "Exactly. All of us. I was hoping I could send Wes off packing today, but if it's still snowing, there's no way he can leave."

"I'm not so sure you'd have an easy time getting him to leave under any circumstances. He really does seem taken with Brenda."

"And she with him," Casey added with a concerned sigh. "As if I didn't have enough problems. Wes can be very engaging. He's good-looking, successful at what he does, and he has a kind of boyish charm that can be quite appealing."

"Appealing enough for you to have married him," John pointed out. "So what happened? Did the charm wear off?"

"No. It wore thin." She tossed the comment off with a wry smile, hoping to put an end to the discussion of her failed marriage.

"Thinning charm. That was what you put down as grounds for divorce?" John persisted.

"I told you last night, we both wanted the divorce," she said, her tone stiffening. "I don't think the details are any of your business."

"Why darling, I thought you told Akiko we don't keep secrets from each other."

"Don't be glib, John. It's not attractive."

"I'm not being glib. I think certain details about Carpenter's moral character and behavior are my business, considering that my ex-wife is currently falling under the spell of his boyish charm."

Casey's eyes narrowed. "And that bothers you. You're jealous?"

"No, it doesn't bother me. If he's right for her and she's right for him . . . great. I'm all for it. But if there's some reason I should be warning Brenda off Carpenter, I'd like to know."

"Don't be ridiculous. Wes is terrific."

"So how come you wanted to split from a terrific guy?"

Instead of answering John, she quirked a brow. "Maybe I'm the one who should be warning Wes about your ex-wife. What was the matter with Brenda, anyway? She's attractive, seems intelligent. Was there something wrong with her character? Her moral fiber?"

"Nothing was wrong with Brenda. Nothing *is* wrong with Brenda. She's a terrific woman. The greatest. The best."

"Well, you don't have to scream her praises."

"I'm not the one who's screaming—you are. Wes told me you had a hot temper. In fact, he hinted that that was one of the reasons the two of you—"

"I do not have a hot temper. I happen to be a very even-tempered person," she replied in a tightly controlled voice.

"And one who doesn't rattle easily," he added, with a sarcastic smirk.

"Talk about charm wearing out," she said acidly, flinging off her covers and getting out of bed on the side away from where John was perched.

He watched her rise. "You know what I think, Casey?"

"I don't care what you think." She started to reach for her *yukata*, but deliberately picked up her flannel robe, instead, and put it on over her nightgown. She looked around in vain for her slippers, finally having to get down on her hands and knees to search for them under her bed.

John's head appeared under the other end of the bed. They simultaneously reached for her slippers, which were lying under the middle of the bed. John managed to get one, Casey the other. Staring at her under the bed he said, "Well, I'm going to tell you what I think, anyway. I think we're having our first marital squabble." He spoke with infuriating equanimity.

"Will you give me my slipper?" she demanded.

He gave a crooked smile, instead. "How about if we finish our fight in the bed instead of under it?"

"John," she warned.

"Yes, darling?"

"Is it too much to ask you to let me preserve a little of my dignity?"

"I think you'd preserve it better if you got off all fours."

At that moment Casey hated John Gallagher. With as much dignity as she could muster, Casey rose to her feet, put on her one slipper and marched to the bathroom. She walked right past the matching slipper John tossed over to her.

As she stepped into the bathroom, ignoring the icy chill of the ceramic tile under her one bare foot, the snooze alarm went off. "'All is calm, all is bright . . .'"

"Bah, humbug," she shouted, slamming the door.

Standing under the hot spray of the shower, Casey tried hard to regain her composure. Quick flashes of the previous day and night thwarted her attempt. Her mind kept filling up with embarrassing freeze-frames.

When she returned to her bedroom ten minutes later, John was gone, his *yukata* neatly folded over hers on her chaise. She looked into the alcove. The bed was folded up. John's clothes weren't there. He must have gotten dressed and gone downstairs, Casey decided.

Or—her stomach gave a sickening lurch—gone—gone, period. Of all the dumb things she'd done, getting into a fight with John had to have been the dumbest. She couldn't afford an argument with John. she needed him. He was the key to pulling off the deal with Matoki. If John had gone, what would she tell Matoki? How would she explain? She couldn't come clean. She'd let things go too far. On the other hand, how would it look to Matoki if she told him she and John had had a marital squabble and he'd walked out on her?

Casey's head started to throb, but she forced herself not to panic. Not yet, anyway.

After throwing on a red turtleneck sweater and navy wool slacks, then tugging on socks and slipping her feet into her loafers, she hurried downstairs.

Wes was in the kitchen making himself a pot of tea when Casey flew in.

"Have you seen John?" she asked breathlessly.

Wes shrugged. "Nope. Maybe he's in the living room with the Matokis."

"Oh, no. They're up already"

"Akiko made coffee," he said, looking up to discover Casey already gone.

Please be in the living room, John. Please. Please.

"Ah, good morning, Casey," Akiko said cheerfully, rising from the couch and giving her hostess a polite bow of greeting. "I hope you do not mind that I made coffee. I saw you had a Japanese coffee maker exactly like mine, and I do enjoy a cup of coffee when I rise."

"Coffee?" Casey muttered distractedly, looking around the empty room. "No, thanks." She focused nervously back on the petite woman dressed in a simple gray wool sweater and tweed skirt.

"Is something wrong, Casey?"

"Wrong? Oh, no. I was just looking for John. He must have woken up early this morning. You haven't seen him, have you? He isn't with your husband by any chance?" Maybe Toho was consulting John on the construction of the "hut" he was supposed to be building come spring.

"Toho is in your den doing his morning Aikido and meditation."

"Alone?"

Akiko smiled. "Oh, yes. Always. He is most private about such rituals."

Casey managed a weak nod. Then she had another thought that gave her a bit of hope. John could be upstairs having a chat with Brenda. Yes, that made sense. That made a lot of sense.

Casey had barely finished the thought, when she heard footsteps behind her.

"Good morning, ladies," Brenda said cheerily as she entered the living room.

Casey slowly looked over her shoulder in Brenda's direction. Brenda was alone.

Casey tried to calm down. Maybe John had stayed upstairs after having his chat with his ex.

"Looks like we're snowed in for the day. I hope you've stocked the larders, Case," Brenda said airily.

Case. Only Wes called her Case.

"There's plenty of food . . . Bren."

"Great, 'cause I'm starving. It must be the weather."

Akiko's dark eyes sparkled like coal. "Or maybe it is love."

Brenda smiled a Cheshire cat smile. "So, anyone else up?"

"Wes is in the kitchen," Akiko supplied.

"And Toho's in the den meditating," Casey added. I haven't seen David yet. And John . . ." She hesitated, hoping Brenda would supply the rest of the sentence. But Brenda's expression was blank. Casey tried for a note of nonchalance. "John's around the house somewhere."

"Oh, no," Akiko said pleasantly. "I saw him leave the house a few minutes ago."

"He . . . left?" The reality hit Casey with a wallop.

"I called out to him, but he did not hear me," Akiko said.

"I wonder where he went," Brenda mused. "Well, I think I'll go get something to eat in the kitchen."

Casey was oblivious to Brenda's departure. Her mind was racing, panic flooding her. But where could he go in this snowstorm? Then she remembered. John's car and his clothes were next door at the Foster house. He probably went there to pack. And try to dig himself out. That could take quite a while with all the snow that had fallen and the blizzard still in progress. If she hurried . . . If she begged him to forgive her . . . got down on her hands and knees . . .

She pulled herself up short. What had happened to her dignity, to her self-respect?

Her mouth set in a firm line. Did she want self-respect or a husband?

"Casey? Are you all right?" Akiko asked. "You look pale."

Casey's hands went absently to her face. "Oh, I'm fine. Just fine. But I...I just remembered something...I have to do. I'll be . . . right back." Without another word she fled from the living room and began racing blindly down the hall toward the front door.

She didn't see Toho Matoki, newly refreshed from his morning exercise and meditation, step out of the den and into the hall, until she collided with him.

They both let out heavy grunts, Toho stumbling back against the wall. Casey quickly righted him and showered him with apologies as she grabbed her coat off the hall tree and pulled open the front door.

"I'm so . . . sorry. I've got to shovel . . . the roof. Danger of . . . falling ice . . . The poor postman . . . We lost one...that way...just last winter." She slammed the door shut, too upset even to consider what Toho would make of the bizarre explanation for her abrupt departure.

Pulling her wool coat closed, Casey wished, after ten steps down the walk, that she'd taken an extra moment to slip on boots. Over a foot of snow had fallen and the drifts were much higher. She was trekking through the frigid mess in her leather loafers, the cold numbing her feet and legs. To make matters worse, vigorous gusts of wind were mixing with the heavy snow, battering and blinding her as she forged on to the Foster house, a good hundred-yard hike from her place.

Casey forgot about the numbing cold as she came in sight of the house. Panic shot through her when she didn't see a car parked out front. But as she got closer, she spotted a high mound of snow in the shape of the car that was buried under it.

She let out a cry of relief and tried to move faster, but her frozen legs gave way and she stumbled face forward into a snow drift. She was covered with snow from head to toe when she finally reached the front door.

With frozen fingers, Casey tested the doorknob. It gave way just as she started to push, and she went flying into the house, landing flat on her face—a position that was getting to seem habitual.

"What have we here? Frosty the Snowman come to play?"

Casey gritted her teeth and looked up through icicle-lashed eyes at John. Let him tease her. Let him have his fun. Let him say whatever he wants. Only let him stay.

John shut the door against the snowy blast and moved to her side. He shook his head and knelt down to help her up. "Good heavens, Casey, didn't your mother teach you to dress properly for a blizzard? No boots, no gloves. You could come down with pneumonia."

"Oh, John, don't go away. Please come back to my house. I'm sorry we had that stupid fight. It was my fault. I . . . I shouldn't have been so . . . so . . ."

"Hot tempered?"

She swallowed a medicinal dose of pride. "Right. Hot tempered."

He grinned. "Come into the den. There are some blankets in there. We'll risk a small fire in the fireplace and see if we can get your teeth to stop chattering."

No wonder she was having so much trouble gritting her teeth. They *were* chattering. She'd been so busy groveling she hadn't even realized.

"I know I had no business . . . getting snappy," Casey went on, letting him escort her into a small wood-paneled den off the hall and over to a couch near the fireplace. After he stripped off her snow-caked wool coat, he sat her down and removed her sodden loafers and socks.

"Your feet look awful," John muttered, lifting them up on the couch and then covering Casey with a couple of plaid wool blankets.

"Just a while ago you said I had great feet." She cracked a little smile. "Feets of wonder."

Smiling back, John tucked the blankets under her heels. "I can't figure you out, Casey."

Her teeth continued to chatter and she was shivering. "I'm . . . easy."

John was at the fireplace. He looked back over his shoulder and gave Casey a Gable grin. "I know," he said with a wink.

"To figure out . . . I mean."

He laughed. "That, too."

"You're really loving this, aren't you, Mr. John Gallagher?"

"That's Mr. John Croyden to you, Mrs. Croyden."

Casey took another swallow of pride. A couple more swallows and she'd be choking. "I . . . I don't want to fight."

"Marriage would be dull without a squabble here and there."

Casey pulled the blankets up to her neck. She couldn't stop shivering.

After a few false starts, John got a fire going. Smoke poured out at first, but it soon cleared.

Within a few minutes the room started warming up. John pushed the sofa closer to the fire, then found a crystal decanter of cognac in one of the cupboards. He splashed some into a water glass, inadvertently half filling it, and brought the drink over to Casey, who was still shivering under the covers.

Casey protestd. "It's ten o'clock in the morning. I...haven't even...had my...coffee...yet," she stammered. "I just...brushed my...teeth."

"Drink it," John ordered, putting the glass to her lips.

Casey took a sip, coughed, and then urged on by John, took several more swallows, each one going down easier than the last. John started to pull the oversize drink away, figuring Casey had had enough, but she held on to his wrist and drank some more.

"Take it easy," John cautioned. "It's morning, remember? And you haven't eaten anything yet."

"Are you afraid I'll get drunk, Mr. Gallagher? Correction. Mr. Croyden?" she asked after downing a good two-thirds of the cognac, greatly enjoying the warming sensation coursing through her body. Her teeth had stopped chattering and the shivers had abated. After a moment, she polished off the rest of the drink.

"That depends. What kind of a drunk are you?"

"I don't know. I've never been drunk in my life." She extended her empty glass. "More, please."

John shook his head and took the glass from her hands. "You've had more than enough. That was a good triple you downed."

He sat on the end of the couch and lifted Casey's feet, covers and all, up on his lap. Slipping his hands under the blankets, he begun gently kneading her still-icy toes.

"Oooh," she moaned.

"Am I hurting you?"

"Oh, no. That feels . . . good." So did the radiant heat from the fire. And the warm glow inside her from the cognac. Casey felt herself start to relax, and she let her head drop back on the arm of the couch. She sighed a bit drunkenly.

"Feeling better?"

"Ummm." The room started to spin a little and Casey closed her eyes. "I guess the truth is I always did have a hot temper. Even as a kid. I was an only child and my parents spoiled me rotten. I got used to having things my own way."

"Was that Wes's gripe?" John said.

"I . . . I can be unreasonable. And I'm bossy. Wes felt I put my needs first all the time."

"Was he right?"

Casey tried to open her eyes, but the spinning had increased. She closed them again. "Work, especially. That always bothered Wes. My work is very important to me. But it's also very pressured. I need to blow off steam a lot, which Wes resented in particular. He wanted a woman who would devote a lot of time to him and his needs. I guess I was . . . a lousy wife."

"Did you ever think, maybe, you just married the wrong guy?"

Casey started to shake her head, but it made her feel queasy. "Wes is a wonderful guy. He's so kind, so sweet, so even tempered, so good-natured."

"Sounds perfect."

Casey sighed. "Well, actually Wes is a little boring. We were good friends before we got married. And luckily we're good friends again. But as husband and wife we were a terrible mishmash . . . I mean, mismatch."

She lifted her head up a few inches and squinted at John. "I'm having trouble focusing."

John smiled. "You're a cheap drunk, anyway."

"I'm not drunk. I'm just a little...giddy." She hiccupped.

John's smile deepened. "I like you giddy."

"You do?"

"I like you not giddy, too."

"You do?"

"This can't be love, can it?"

Casey stared at his double image. "Oh, no. It can't be love. That would be so...inconvenient."

He laughed softly, his hands skimming up her calves. "Oh, Casey, Casey. I don't know what this is I'm feeling, but I can tell you one thing. I've never felt this way before."

"Not even with Brenda?" Casey shivered, but this time it had nothing to do with being cold.

"The truth is, life with Brenda was kind of dull, too."

Casey giggled. "Well, we can't say that about our marriage."

John gave her one last caress and drew his hands away.

"Oh, don't stop. That feels so good. I want you to ..." She gave him a lopsided smile and made a grab for his hand. "I want you."

John brought her hand to his lips. "Tell me that again when you're sober."

Casey let her head drop back on the arm of the sofa. "Okay, darling."

A few minutes later, Casey squinted at John. "I think I must be drunk. I'm...hearing things. The pitter-patter of ..." She frowned. "Of reindeer?" She leaned her head back and giggled. "Do you suppose it could be...Rudolf, the red-nosed reindeer leading Donner and Blitzen and . . . oh, I can't remember the rest."

"Casey, it isn't Rudolf," John said in a low voice, his eyes, not on her but on the red nose of Toho Matoki who was leading a pack—not of reindeer—but of house-guests, all of whom had anxious looks on their faces.

Casey struggled to a sitting position and gave the new, snow-covered arrivals a tipsy smile.

"The door was unlocked," Brenda said apologeti-cally. "We were worried."

"We thought at first," Toho said severely, "you might have fallen from the roof."

John gave Casey a bemused look. "The roof?"

Casey shrugged.

"You said you had to shovel snow from your roof. Be-cause of the postman, I believe you said," Toho contin-ued grimly. "When you did not return, we all searched the grounds around the house, fearing that you had fallen."

"Oh," Casey muttered. "Fallen from grace. What an awful thought."

"Where does the postman fit in, darling?" John asked.

Casey had to think for a moment. "Oh, yes. The post-man. Through rain, snow and sleet. But falling ice...now that's beyond the call of duty."

"Aha," John said with an understanding nod. Then he turned to Toho and friends. "I can explain. You see, I came over here to check on our neighbor's house. We do that for each other. And then Casey came over to get a shovel. The Fosters had borrowed it last time they were up."

Casey giggled. "Oh, John, you're so clever. You're saving my neck again."

John smiled. "Well, darling, it's a very pretty neck."

"Thank you."

There were a few titters from the group. Toho, however, didn't crack a smile. "Have you been drinking, Casey?"

Casey hiccuped and put her hand to her lips. "Oh, how rude of me." Her hand left her mouth and made a sweeping arc. "Darling, drinks for everyone," she said grandly.

A moment later she passed out cold.

7

Jingle all the way...

CASEY AWOKE WITH A JOLT. The room was dark. She had no idea what time it was. Actually, she wasn't even sure what bed she was in. Propping herself up on one elbow, she tried to ignore the pounding in her head and her sandpaper-dry throat as she flicked on the bedside light, shading her eyes from the sudden harsh glare.

Well, she was in her own room, in her own bed, wearing her own nightgown. How she got there and got undressed was another question. Last thing she could remember, she was wearing slacks and a turtleneck and she was looking frantically for her missing "husband."

Her throbbing head fell back on the pillow as Casey let out a low moan. No, that wasn't quite the last thing she remembered. She remembered finding John next door. She remembered he'd given her some brandy because her teeth were chattering. She remembered how the brandy had stopped her teeth from chattering and how it gave her such a delicious warm feeling. Then she remembered the lovely reconciliation she and John were right in the middle of . . . when the reindeer arrived.

Only, Casey remembered, they weren't reindeer . . .

She moaned again, this time louder. It seemed to her at that moment that some people had all the luck and some people had none. Until yesterday she'd always seen herself as a member of the first category. But then the twisted hand of fate had abruptly decided enough was enough and had shoved her, without warning, into the dumpster.

Nothing, absolutely nothing had gone right for Casey since she'd embarked on this harebrained scheme. Once again, freeze-frame images appeared before her eyes. Then when she shut her eyes, the stern image of Toho Matoki loomed in her mind. She realized now that Matoki's face was the last thing she could recall before everything went blank. She could even hear his voice. He was asking her something. What was it?

She let out a symphony of groans as she remembered exactly what it was.

"Oh, no," she thought with despair, realizing that now Matoki must not only think her a screwball, but even worse, a screwball with a drinking problem.

There was a soft rap on her door. Casey didn't answer, hoping whoever it was would go away. What she really hoped was that the floor would open beneath her and just swallow her up. She felt too humiliated to face anyone ever again, especially Toho Matoki.

The door cracked open before Casey could reach out her hand to flick off the light and pretend to still be asleep.

"You're up." Brenda stepped into the room and shut the door behind her. "How do you feel?"

Casey couldn't respond. She had all she could do to keep from bursting into tears.

"Dinner's almost ready. Do you feel up to eating?"

"Dinner?" Casey squinted at the clock. Six-twenty. "Did I sleep all day?"

Brenda smiled. "Most of it."

Casey put her hands to her eyes.

"You should come down and eat something. Akiko did the cooking. With John's help. A hearty stew. Smells divine. And Wes thought after supper we could roast chestnuts."

"I don't want to eat. I'm sick."

Brenda gave Casey a sympathetic smile. "Can I bring you something? Alka-Seltzer?"

Casey shook her head. "Not that kind of sick," she muttered, tears spilling from her eyes.

"It's not so bad," Brenda said. "Really."

"It is so bad. And what's even worse—" Casey hesitated, giving Brenda a sideways glance before throwing her arm across her eyes "—I think I'm somewhat...infatuated with your ex-husband." she swallowed hard and licked her dry lips. Her head hurt so badly.

Brenda smiled. "Even for an ex-husband, John's a very appealing guy."

Casey let the arm covering her eyes drop to her side. "But he wasn't appealing enough for you." The statement held a definite questioning note.

Brenda looked uncomfortable. "Appeal alone doesn't make a marriage, Casey. It takes...more than that."

"What was missing?" Casey asked.

Brenda gave an awkward laugh. "Look, Casey, if what you want are my blessings, you've got them. John and I just didn't mesh. We're too different. John's very high-powered, very dynamic, incredibly clever and urbane. I'm just a simple soul, with simple interests, simple needs. I'm sure I seemed dull to John, although he was always too kind to put it that way. We...rushed into something, realized it was a mistake and got out while we could still like each other." She released a long breath. "There, does that tell you what you want to know?"

Casey smiled faintly. "Thanks, Brenda. Thanks for everything. You've been such a good sport. And it's all been such a complete disaster."

Brenda's hazel eyes sparkled. "I wouldn't say that."

"You really do like Wes, don't you?"

"He seems so tender, kind, good-natured, easygoing. Almost too good to be true."

Casey, for all her own misery, managed a warm smile. "Believe it, it's true. Wes is everything you think and more." And then, before Brenda could ask, Casey went on, "But even tender, kind and easygoing don't make a marriage. I hope it works out for you and Wes, Brenda. I think the two of you would make a great pair."

"You mean that, Casey?"

"Absolutely."

Brenda shrugged. "Well, time will tell. It has been pretty crazy around here. And then there's the romantic mood and magic of Christmas in Vermont. Who can be sure what's real anymore?"

Casey sighed heavily. "Some of it is too real to think about."

"You mean Matoki?"

Casey shut her eyes and nodded.

"Don't worry about Matoki. John had a long heart to heart with him. I even heard Matoki laughing."

Casey shot up to a sitting position, forgetting all about her pounding head. "Laughing?"

"That's got to be a good sign, right?"

Casey was out of bed, pulling off her nightgown and throwing on some clothes. "Not if he was laughing at me." A wave of panic went through her. What if John had taken it upon himself to tell Matoki the truth?

"I'll go tell them you'll be joining us for dinner then, okay?"

"I may be the dinner," Casey muttered despondently as she faced herself in the mirror and saw that she looked as awful as she felt.

By the time she started downstairs, Casey's head was throbbing even more, and her stomach felt like a dryer with a pair of tennis sneakers banging around in it. To make matters worse, as she hit the bottom step, Toho Matoki stepped out of the den into the hall.

Casey opened her mouth to speak, but nothing came out. She really had no idea what to say.

Matoki had no such difficulty. After a brief formal bow, he addressed her in a stern voice. "Please, Casey, I would like to have a private word with you in your den."

Casey looked at him balefully but nodded assent. He turned and reentered the den.

Well, it's over and done with, Casey thought as she walked down the hall. John must have told him the truth. *Maybe it's better this way*, she lied to herself.

Casey stepped into the den. Matoki was standing by the fireplace, hands locked in front of him, his dark eyes watching her, unwavering.

"Please, I'd like to explain . . ." Casey started, but Matoki waved her to silence.

"John has already explained."

"But I'd like to tell you myself. I owe at least that much to you. And to your wife. To everyone," she persisted desperately.

"You look pale, Casey. Sit down."

He spoke with such command, she immediately obeyed his order.

When she started to speak from the armchair—the seat that was closest to her—he once again motioned her to be silent.

"I understand fully, Casey. There is no need for you to provide any details. I do not wish to embarrass you."

"I'm so ashamed," she said in a low voice, staring morosely at him. With all hope lost, a numbing sensation seemed to take hold of her mind and body.

Matoki came over and looked down at her. "You may find this hard to believe, but I do understand what you're going through. Indeed, I've been through it myself."

"You've been through it yourself?"

"I once had a similar problem with alcohol and pills."

This conversation was getting very strange. "Similar to who . . . to whom?"

He gave her a sympathetic smile. "It is merely something to be aware of. Something one must take caution against. Do not be so hard on yourself over a simple error in judgment."

"Believe me, it's never happened before. I don't even like alcohol. A glass of wine or two . . . at the most. And never, never in the morning. And as far as pills are concerned, I've never . . ."

"Yes, I know. John has explained all that. And as for this other business concerning you and John, Casey, it happens. To the best of us."

"John told you . . . everything?"

Toho took hold of her hand. "He was most discreet in the telling. But he explained enough for me to get a fair picture, shall I say?"

"And you don't . . . hold it against me?"

He squeezed her hand before releasing it. "Not in the least. Indeed, I admire you, Casey. You don't sit back and allow yourself to be manipulated."

Casey couldn't believe her ears. Matoki knew the truth and he was forgiving her? He understood? He sympathized? He admired her? Was she dreaming?

He rested a hand on her shoulder. "Do not take it to heart. At times such as this we must bend like the tree. That is crucial in life, whether in one's business or one's personal affairs."

Casey could only look up at Matoki with wide eyes, her mouth dropped open in amazement.

He smiled down at her. Yes, he actually smiled. It quite transformed his face. Gone was the grim, forbidding set to his features. He looked almost endearing. Casey felt tears start to trickle down her cheeks.

"I don't know what to say," she murmured, unable to meet his gaze. "I swear to you, this isn't the way I usually operate. I've never... It's just that...I wanted things to go well. I...had such a wonderful scheme." She blanched. "I mean . . . for your new hotel chain. I . . ."

"I know a little about your scheme."

Casey's eyes shot up. "You do?"

"John's told me a bit."

Casey closed her eyes. Yes, John had told him all right. A part of her felt angry and betrayed. After all, John had no right to take it upon himself to spill the beans. Yet how could she really be angry when Matoki was standing here before her filled with understanding and forgiveness? And the best part was, she was off the hook. The ruse was over. She could go back to being . . . normal.

But, would she ever be quite normal again?

"I'm very impressed with John," Toho was saying. "He is clear thinking, creative, shrewd. I like the way he expresses himself. Which is not to say his comments in any way diminish your proposal. Quite the contrary. His views greatly enhance your ideas."

Casey was getting lost again. "My proposal?"

"Yes. Of course, John only gave me a broad overview, but I was impressed."

Casey was wondering whether the stuporous effects of the cognac had fully left her system. She felt dazed. "Wait a second. Are you saying that John gave you a broad overview of *my* Japanese-American hotel proposal for your company?"

"As well as presenting some very practical and innovative comments of his own. His experience working in Japan has given him a special insider's perspective. But he did make it absolutely clear that the proposal was yours alone and that he wants none of the credit. He was quite insistent about that." Toho's grim expression returned. "I sincerely hope, Casey, this won't be cause for another—how did John put it—lovebirds' squabble?"

Casey stared up at Toho Matoki as she tried to fit the pieces of the conversation together. Only they didn't fit. Something was wrong here. Everything was wrong. Nothing was making any sense. If John had come clean, what was all this about lovebirds?

Toho was smiling at her again. "You've got a good man in John, Casey. I have no doubt that he loves you. Nor does Akiko have any doubts. And my wife, I assure you, is a most astute observer of human nature. Rarely have we seen a couple so right for each other as you and John. Do not be too hard on him. Bend like the tree, Casey."

"Bend like the tree?"

"Forget your squabble. John is quite willing to forget about it. He understands that women can be jealous creatures, and perhaps he did tease you a bit too much about Brenda."

"About Brenda? Then he told you about Brenda?"

"What is past is past. What happened once, a long time ago, should not destroy the present. May I tell you something?"

Casey was dumfounded. "Anything."

"I think John's attraction to Brenda was not deep. Certainly not what you imagined it was. A brief interlude."

"It wasn't so brief."

"Ah, time is relative, Casey. For some a moment is everything, and for some days, weeks, years do not fully satisfy."

Casey didn't know what to say. She didn't know what to think. The Eastern mind seemed beyond fathoming.

"And if I may suggest, you should learn to be more relaxed, Casey," Toho went on amiably. "Perhaps I can teach you Aikido and meditation while I am here. It is much better than tranquilizers."

Casey did a double take. "Tranquilizers?" Who was taking tranquilizers?

Toho's expression became solemn. "As I said, I, too, once had a serious reaction from taking medication and then forgetting and enjoying a few glasses of sake. Like you, the powerful combination went right to my head. Although, of course, John took full responsibility for your reaction this morning. He forgot about your tranquilizers when he gave you the brandy to take away the chill from your bones. And, although he did not say, to help calm your ragged nerves. Given the state I myself saw you were in, I might have done the same as him."

Casey was speechless.

Toho pressed his hands together beneath his chin and gave her a paternal smile. "So, shall we go on from here? A nice dinner. And then chestnuts roasting on an open fire. Ah, yes, I know the tune. It is played in Japan. But I have never had chestnuts. I am greatly looking forward to the experience." His smile had almost a whimsical cast. "So many unique experiences for us, my young friend. Akiko and I are most grateful for your delightful hospitality. And as for your proposal, we shall definitely take some time from all the holiday fun for more serious discussion." He took hold of her hand. "And, if you have no objection, John can participate, as well."

"John?"

"You have a most clever and engaging husband, Casey. As Akiko says, a husband to treasure."

"To treasure..." Casey echoed, a dazed expression on her face. A husband to treasure? Then John hadn't told Matoki the truth. All he'd really done for her was make matters worse.

There was a soft rap on the door.

"Casey?" John's voice wafted into the room.

Toho gave her a reassuring pat on the shoulder. "Bend, Casey."

"Like a tree," she said between clenched teeth as Toho went to let John in.

Casey's back was to the door so she didn't see John enter, but she could imagine the two men sharing conspiratorial smiles.

The next minute John was smiling sheepishly down at her. "So, darling, is all forgiven?"

Casey manufactured a smile for Toho's benefit.

John knelt in front of her. "We should never have squabbled over that dumb weekend when Brenda and Wes came up. I admit, maybe I did flirt with her a little. But more to make you jealous than anything else. Like I told Toho here, it was harmless. and as Toho can vouch, I've hardly given Brenda a look since she came up this time. Really, darling, there's absolutely no reason for you to doubt my feelings for you. I'm crazy about you, Casey. You're the only woman for me. If I had any doubts before, I have absolutely none now."

Toho gave a satisfied sigh. "Said with sincerity and honesty, John."

"Thank you, Toho," John said gratefully before fully returning his attentions to Casey. "And as for your blacking out from the brandy this morning, darling, I explained to Toho about—"

"About the tranquilizers?"

"You're upset about the tranquilizers. Of course you're upset. You probably didn't want me to mention them."

"You could put it that way."

"She's a very proud woman, Toho. But, then, who better than a Japanese to understand about losing face."

"But you have not lost face, Casey," Toho insisted. "Indeed, I feel indirectly responsible for your present emotional state."

"What?" Casey asked, astonished by the remark.

"Yes, yes. Once John explained that most of your work and the stress you've been under has revolved around your proposal for my Japanese-American hotel chain, I felt quite responsible." He paused. "On the positive side, I am intrigued by your ideas. And yours, as well, John."

"Which ideas have you shared, darling?" Casey's brows arched in a large question mark.

"Nothing much."

"You are too modest, John. Granted, you have no direct hotel experience, but you have a quality that is equally valuable—a shrewd business sense. And, even more important, you have a surprisingly astute understanding of Japanese tastes and style. As I said to you, Casey, we would do well to include your husband in on our talk about your proposal. Perhaps, between the three of us, we might come up with just the right blend of ingredients."

John took hold of Casey's hand and brought it to his lips. Casey had no recourse but to allow the intimacy since Toho was watching from the doorway.

"Please don't think I'm butting in, darling. All I was trying to do was help you," he crooned.

"Well," Toho said brightly, "I shall make a discreet leave so that the two of you can have a proper reconciliation." Before he left he turned back to Casey. "Tomorrow morning, Casey, I shall give you your first lesson in aikido and meditation."

"What's that about?" John asked after Toho left.

"So much healthier than popping tranquilizers," Casey replied acidly.

John grinned. "I thought the tranquilizers were a nice touch. It was either that or have Matoki know you'd downed a tumbler of cognac like it was a milkshake."

"Nice touch? Nice touch?" Casey leaped out of her chair, her movement so abrupt that John, still on his knees, fell backward onto his rear end.

She swung around and glared down at him. "How could you? How could you do it?" Casey ranted, coming back to life with a vengeance.

"Why do I get the feeling this isn't the prelude to a thank-you, darling?"

"Thank you? Thank you for what? For making me out to be a jealous shrew who pops tranquilizers on top of being a screwball? And to make matters even worse, half the time Matoki was lecturing me before you arrived, telling me to bend like a tree and about how you and Brenda were nothing more than a . . . a brief interlude, I was thinking you'd told him the truth. I thought he knew about your marriage to Brenda. I thought he knew about us. I thought he was forgiving me for the insane ruse I'd created." She squeezed her eyes shut. "I've never been so humiliated." She emitted a low moan. "What am I saying? I've been in a more or less constant state of humiliation since I first set eyes on the Matokis. And here you are, weaving tales of jealousy and drugs. This can't be happening to me."

John rose to his feet and took hold of Casey's wrist.

"Let go of me. Can't you see what you've done?"

He refused to release his hold. Quite the contrary, he pulled her roughly to him. "What I've done, my darling wife, is save your pretty neck. A neck, I might add, I've grown quite fond of."

"I suppose that's why you stuck it in a noose."

"What noose? Didn't you hear a word Matoki said? He likes your proposal."

"And that's another thing. How do you know anything about my proposal?"

"You left the file lying open on the floor beside your bed. I was curious to see how good you were at what you do. You kept making such a point of work being your whole life. So I read it. And guess what? I was damned impressed. You are good, Casey. You're creative and daring without sacrificing the economic end. And Matoki thinks you're good, too. Isn't that what you wanted? Isn't that what this is all about?"

John's argument brought Casey up short. She stared at him thoughtfully. She'd gotten so caught up in her feelings, she was missing the big picture. What John said was true. He had swung Matoki over to her corner. Instead of disaster, he'd actually performed a miracle and turned everything around. Once she looked beyond the additional dose of humiliation and embarrassment, she had to admit John's intimate little heart to heart with Toho, while outlandish, was a brilliant stroke.

Before she could eat humble pie, John spoke. "And another thing you ought to know," he said, slipping his arms around her waist. "I wasn't running out on you this morning. Even if I were, how far do you think I'd have gotten in that blizzard?"

"There are a dozen houses or more before the bridge. Who wouldn't take in a handsome stranded traveler like you?"

He laughed softly. "But who else would invite me to play her husband?" As he spoke his hands followed the line of her body from her waist down over her hips. "And what other woman could ever be so exciting and entrancing in the role of my wife?"

Casey drew a shaky breath. "Oh, John, there seems to be no end to the fool I can make of myself."

"It's not turning out so bad though, is it?" John's voice was whisper soft.

Her heart fluttered. "No. No, it isn't. Actually, this could turn out to be the best Christmas of my life."

There was a soft rap on the door. "Dinner's ready," Brenda called through the closed door. There was a moment's hesitation. "Shall we go on without you?"

Casey's eyes met John's and held. "Yes, go ahead, Brenda," she called back. "We'll join you later... for chestnuts."

John's right hand reached toward Casey's face. His fingertips brushed her cheek, her temple, slid through her fine blond hair. Casey leaned toward him for their kiss.

"Oh, John," she murmured against his parted lips, "I am intoxicated, infatuated..."

Gently he drew back, observing her with a wry Gable look. "But not inebriated?"

Casey smiled. "I wasn't really all that inebriated this morning when I said I wanted you." Her blue eyes sparkled. "I'm stone sober now." Her hands cupped his face and she kissed him lightly. "And I want you even more," she whispered breathlessly. "What about you? Do you still want me?"

He let his hands answer, stroking her back, her neck, her face. His thumb moved to her mouth. She kissed his palm, his fingertips, slipped each finger in turn between her lips.

His other hand was edging her sweater up, caressing her warm, soft skin beneath. Casey helped him get the sweater over her head.

He was undoing her bra, her hands were at the buttons of his shirt, when she asked, "What will they all think?"

John's mouth curved into a smile. "They'll think the stew is delicious and that we're in the den having a proper reconciliation." He left Casey for a moment to lock the door, then returned and slowly, provocatively, slipped the bra off her shoulders. Then he pressed his lips to her breast, savoring the scent and softness of her skin. His thumb stroked her nipple until it swelled beneath his touch.

As John's lips captured the hardened bud, Casey's breathing grew ragged. She pulled off his shirt and leaned heavily into him, her legs rubbery.

They finished undressing each other, taking it slow, watching, touching, exploring, admiring, tasting. They sank to the carpeted floor, entwined, kissing, both of them feeling a fire and a boneless melting.

"You are incredibly beautiful," John whispered against her mouth, his fingers stroking her neck. His lips moved over the planes of her face. "You're fascinating, tantalizing . . ." He was nibbling her earlobe.

Casey flushed with pleasure and arousal. "Gable doesn't hold a candle to you, John," she murmured as she leaned over him, the tips of her breasts brushing across his broad chest.

His hands were caressing the curves of her hips. "Gable?"

She grinned. "You remind me of him. Right down to that devilish glint in your eye."

He laughed softly.

"What's so funny?" she asked, pressing her lips to his neck, her hands moving down over his taut stomach where a patch of soft hair began, and then lower still.

Shifting, John rolled her onto her back, moving on top of her. "It's funny me reminding you of Gable. It was Gable who talked about the walls of Jericho in that movie *It Happened One Night*. Remember I mentioned it?"

"Yes. You said if we weren't careful the walls would come tumbling down."

John's eyes flashed. "Talk about being careful, I haven't . . ."

Casey's smile was luminous. "I'm on the pill."

He drew her close. "I think I hear Joshua blowing his horn this very moment." His mouth moved over hers in a kiss that started out tender but quickly grew heated and urgent, his tongue possessing her mouth. When he withdrew from her lips, he lowered his head to the peaks of her firm, high breasts, his tongue playing slowly on one taut nipple and then the other.

As Casey writhed beneath John with ragged moans of pleasure, her hands explored his body, its warm hollows, its muscularity, its hardness. She loved his firm, athletic build. She loved his whispered words of pleasure at her caresses. She loved the way he stroked, smoothed and touched her everywhere. Everything else seemed to melt away as she focused on the urgent sensations inside her. He gently parted her thighs. Casey arched to receive him as he entered her.

John covered her with his whole body, thrusting deep inside her, capturing her mouth as they moved together. Casey could feel the heat building and building inside her as he thrust deeper and deeper, their rhythms beginning to match.

John heard Casey cry out beneath his mouth. Clasped in her smooth throbbing warmth, he let himself go, his cry meeting hers.

They lay still, their breathing still ragged, their lips still touching lighter. "Mmmm. What smells so good?" Casey murmured against his mouth.

"Mmmm. You."

Casey wrapped her long legs around his body. Her arms circled his damp back, and she hugged him as tightly as she could. "It's chestnuts. They're roasting chestnuts."

Softly John began crooning, "'Although it's been said many times, many ways . . .'" He stopped, gently rolled off her and propped himself up on one elbow. His finger traced the delicate line of her shapely nose as he finished his rendition. "I'm falling in love with you, Casey."

He sang off-key, and he'd made up the lyrics, but it was the most wonderful Christmas song Casey had ever heard sung.

8

Good King Wenceslas last look'd out . . .

"JOHN?"

"Yes, darling?"

"Is it still snowing?"

"No."

Casey, snuggled in her bed, popped open one eye to greet the new morning. "What do we do now?"

John walked away from the window and crawled back under the covers, his hand cruising over the curve of her hip. "I have one or two ideas."

"No, I mean about Wes and David. How do we make sure they don't put any kinks in the works?"

Casey gave him a crooked smile. "You aren't sticking to the script."

"We make quite a team."

Casey didn't argue. She wanted them to be a team. Even if it was nothing but holiday magic. Even if it didn't last beyond jolly Saint Nick's arrival down the chimney. And if it did last, if miracles did happen, who was she to look a gift miracle in the mouth . . . ?

His hand trailed down her spine and Casey shivered. She stopped further exploration by taking hold of his wrist, her expression earnest as she leveled her gaze at him. "I don't usually do things like this, John."

He kissed the tip of her nose. "Neither do I."

"I almost never do things like this," she emphasized. "In fact, last time I did find myself in this position—" she grinned "—pun intended...I ended up marrying the guy."

"Is that a promise or a warning?"

His hand found its way to Casey's breast and she drew in a breath. "I'm not sure."

He pressed his lips to her hair. "Why don't we see how the honeymoon goes and then figure out the long-term options?"

Casey's blue eyes sparkled. "Another great idea."

"I'm full of them," he whispered, letting his fingertips glide down the valley between her breasts.

Her hands were trembling with excitement as she loosened the neckline of his *yukata*, tracing the carved line of his muscular chest. Then she reached lower and undid the tie of his robe and drew it open, curling her naked body into him so that they were molded into one. "You are wonderful, John."

His tongue drew a warm, moist line along her lips. "And insatiable."

Casey sighed. "It's nearly 9:00 a.m. We should get going."

"I'm working on it," he whispered with a lascivious grin.

Casey laughed as he pressed her tighter to him. "You're a hard worker, John Gallagher."

"That's John Croyden, remember?"

Casey nuzzled her face into his neck. "No. Not here. Not now when it's just the two of us alone. I want this to be real. Straight from the heart."

He put his hands on either side of her face and kissed her lips very gently. "Does that feel real?"

"Mmmm."

He slid his palms down her back, over her firm, rounded buttocks. "And this . . . does this feel real?"

Her "mmmm" was more a breathy sigh.

"And this?" One hand snaked between their tightly molded bodies and down her flat belly.

"Oh, John, that's wonderful." Her breath caught as his hand moved lower, and his fingers began to stroke, circle, probe. She closed her eyes, losing herself in the sensations coursing through her.

When his mouth moved over hers, their kiss was raw with hunger. His tongue slipped silkily past her lips, and as the kiss deepened, Casey could feel a ribbon of fever along her whole body, her rapid pulse melding with his. She reached between them, caressing him, encircling him, moving her hand in a gentle rhythm. A groan escaped his lips as they kissed, and she could feel the vibrations in her mouth.

John's palms slid over her breasts. The skin was satin smooth, warm, the nipples hard and sensitive. Casey gave a little cry when his thumbs brushed against them. But when he went to draw his hands away, her own hands moved over his, and she pressed his palms tight to her breasts.

"Casey," he whispered, feeling the urgency build in him like a fast-ticking bomb. His strong hands moved from her breasts down her rib cage, over her accentuated hipbones. He drew her gently from him so that he could feast his eyes on her exquisite body. "I'll tell you one thing, Casey, in all my thirty-four years, Santa has never been this good to me. You are the best wrapped package a guy could ask for. And what's inside the wrapping is out of this world."

She gave him a look that was part mischief, part passion. "You make a pretty good surprise present yourself." She boldly surveyed him, first with her eyes, then her hands and finally her mouth, her tongue trailing a heated path downward. She caressed him with utter sensuousness and natural abandon, thrilling to the feel of him, the taste of him, loving the way he gasped with pleasure. She could feel the ripple of his muscles as her hands stroked him.

When she'd left her mark on every inch of him, he drew her back up and captured her lips, slipping his hands down over her hips, pulling her closer. He lifted her hair and pressed his mouth to the side of her neck just below her ear. Casey could hear his breath coming in short, uneven gasps. Her own breathing was rapid and shallow as a wave of heat spread through her body. His lips caught her earlobe, his fingers tangling in her hair. He rolled her onto her back, his full weight pressing her into the mattress. Casey arched into him, pressing her hips closer.

His fingers dug into the soft skin of her thighs as Casey's legs encircled him. She whispered his name over and over as she felt him filling her. John looked down at her, taking a greedy delight in watching desire and passion and hunger for him play across her face.

Her eyelids fluttered open, an intoxicating smile curving her lips. "Kiss me, John." And then she emitted a low, catlike growl. "Now, now..."

He covered her mouth with his own, kissing her fiercely, driving inside of her, feeling her shuddering release, making it one with his own.

Afterward, she lay in his arms, his lips pressed to her hair, his hands idly stroking her back, her arms, the curve of her hip.

"Mmmm. This is the second best part," she murmured, sucking in a breath as his hand drifted down to her thigh.

He kissed the corners of her lips. "Does this mean you aren't sorry anymore that I arrived at your front door before David Quinn?"

Casey laughed. "Well, he could have taught me the method approach."

John gave her a slap on her rear.

"Okay, okay. I'm not sorry. I'm glad. I'm ecstatic." She hesitated, lifting her eyes to his. "I think . . . I'm falling in love with you."

He smiled rakishly and held her gaze. "Even though it's terribly inconvenient?"

Casey arched a brow. "Maybe it isn't so inconvenient."

John gave her a shrewd look, his hands moving to circle her waist. "What does that mean?"

She drew her head back. "We do make a good team." Her fingers smoothed his dark tousled hair. "Toho was very impressed with your comments on my proposal. And you said yourself, you're presently . . . unemployed."

John's expression grew warier. "By choice. I needed a break."

Casey's eyes sparkled. "This could be your lucky break."

He grinned. "It's already been luckier than I could have imagined."

"Why should it end? This could be a new beginning for you."

"Somehow I don't think we're walking through a winter wonderland anymore. I feel like we've suddenly caught a rush-hour express to Manhattan." His tone held a definite edge.

Casey fluffed her pillows and sat up, drawing the cover modestly over her breasts. "I could use help on this project with Toho, John. I thought you might want to . . ."

"Be your assistant? That's what you were going to say, isn't it?"

"Oh, now I see. It isn't talking about work that bothers you. It's the idea of my being the one on top."

John chuckled. "You can be on top anytime you like, darling," he drawled.

Casey could feel her temper mounting. "In bed, but not in the office. How quaint."

"I don't want to work for you, Casey."

"Work under me, you mean. I thought we'd come out of the Dark Ages, but I guess some of us haven't. Maybe you spent too much time working in Japan. Women in this country, believe it or not, actually do more than type and take dictation. Some of us, myself included, actually have fairly prestigious positions."

"You've got some great positions, Casey. No argument there."

"Oh, I see what you're doing. I see it all very clearly."

"You do?"

"Your ego can't handle it. You're insecure and you cover it up with glib sexual innuendo."

"Correct me if I'm wrong, but a few minutes ago I thought we were engaging in more than innuendo."

"That's right. Bring it all down to sex. And I thought you were so clever, so strong, so sure of yourself. I actually thought we could be a team."

"You don't want a team. You want a flunky." He flung the covers off and got out of bed. "I'm beginning to see what your ex-husband was talking about. If this is the kind of afterglow Wes experienced, no wonder he got fed up and walked out."

Casey kicked the covers back and shot out of bed after him. "He did not get fed up. And for your information, we had plenty of afterglow. And I'll tell you something else. I can handle Matoki just fine without your help, thank you. You're the one who's out of a job. I was just trying to help you."

"Believe me, Casey, it'll be a cold day in hell before I need your help."

"Well, hell will freeze over before I ever offer it again."

A soft rap on the door abruptly halted their screaming match and prompted the realization that they were facing off stark naked.

"Yes?" Casey called out in a syrupy voice as she made a dash for her robe.

"Good morning, Casey."

Casey blanched. It was Toho Matoki. He had to have heard them arguing.

"Relax," John whispered, reading her mind. "Plenty of married couples have a spat a day."

Casey scowled at him as she rushed over to get his *yukata*, which was crumpled up under the covers. She tossed it at him, gave him a beseeching look and then went to open the door.

Toho Matoki stood in the hall wearing a short white kimono and matching trousers. He eyed Casey with a somber expression. "I always prefer exercise before breakfast."

John came up behind her. "Oh, so do we, Toho," he said, amusement clear in his voice.

Casey surreptitiously glanced over her shoulder at John, relieved to see that he was wearing his robe.

Meanwhile, the two men were sharing knowing looks.

"I meant to be downstairs by nine o'clock," she said thickly to Toho.

John's arm swung heavily over her shoulder. "Yes, she did."

"We . . . we got caught up in a silly little argument." Casey could feel the heat rising in her cheeks.

Toho observed her closely, much to Casey's consternation and discomfort. His index finger moved to his lips and he tapped rhythmically.

Between Toho's silent survey and John's arm slung over her shoulder, Casey felt the tension building inside her, an explosion imminent.

Finally Toho dropped his hand to his side. "Are you free of all drugs, Casey?"

"Am I . . . what?" she asked, startled.

John gave her an affectionate squeeze. "He means the tranquilizers, darling."

Casey could feel her blood boil. "I assure you, Toho, I have taken no tranquilizers," she said in a clipped tone.

He nodded. "Yes, I see that is true. Tranquilizers would mask your tension."

John stroked Casey's hair, ignoring her rigid stance. "I think she got up on the wrong side of the bed." He laughed softly. "Actually, I think we both did." He looked down at Casey, giving her a teasing smile. "Let's switch sides tomorrow morning, shall we?"

"Yes, let's definitely do something different tomorrow morning," she bit back.

Toho seemed disinterested in their bed rituals. "So, we shall begin in twenty minutes in your den."

Casey was quick to consent. "I'll bring my files."

"Files?"

"What are you thinking, darling? Toho means your introduction in aikido and meditation. Business is never conducted before the morning's rituals."

Casey had completely forgotten about the exercise program Toho was determined to teach her.

John gave her a moist kiss on her cheek. "You couldn't begin at a better time, darling. I just bet you'll feel like a new woman afterward. Don't you think so, Toho?"

Toho crossed his arms over his narrow chest. "In time. In time."

John gave Casey another squeeze, throwing her off balance so that she fell against him. "Oh, I think you'll be surprised, Toho, at what a quick study Casey is."

"A pleasant surprise," replied Toho, "is always most appreciated."

JOHN WAS FINISHING dressing when Wes Carpenter knocked on the door. "If you're looking for Casey," John said amiably, "she's doing aikido with Toho down in the den. I wouldn't disturb them, though. It's a private ritual."

Wes gave John a narrow look and stepped into the bedroom.

"This is getting out of hand. You're sharing Casey's bedroom. She's performing private little rituals in the den with this Oriental fellow. And that Quinn character is driving both me and Brenda up the wall. Right now he's sitting in the kitchen with Akiko, telling her how heartbroken he is about Brenda not giving him the time of day. The guy thinks he's a regular Paul Newman or something."

"Yeah, he's bucking for an Oscar all right," John said, grinning.

"I'll give him an Oscar. Along with a bloody nose, if he makes a grab for Brenda under the table again like he did at dinner last night."

John chuckled. "Sounds like I missed some good action in the dining room."

Wes gave John a stern look. "What I want to know is what kind of action you were getting in the den. Not to mention up here in Casey's bedroom. That's what I want to talk to you about, buddy."

John gave Wes a leery look. "Aren't you getting even the real roles mixed up a bit, Wes? Casey's your *ex* wife. I don't think it's exactly your place to be questioning me about what Casey and I do in any room in this house."

"Ex-wife or not, I happen to care about Casey. And I don't want to see her getting hurt. As far as I can see, Quinn isn't the only one getting carried away with his role around here. Aren't you taking the part of the husband a little too seriously?"

"What about your role as Brenda's lover?"

"Maybe it started out as a role, but Brenda happens to be a terrific woman."

"There, you see. It's the same with me and Casey. Believe me, I wasn't out looking. But Casey... she's something else. She gets right under your skin and digs in."

"I'll tell you something," Wes said in a low, confidential tone. "The...uh...very first time Casey and I moved from being good friends to being more romantically involved, I knew I was going to marry her. It hit me" he thumped his chest "—like that. Casey, too. Although, looking back on it, I was the one who put on the pressure. Casey tried to be sensible, and most of the time she is mighty sensible, but then there are times..."

John's lips curved into a smile. "Yeah, there are those times for all of us."

Wes rubbed his jaw. "Yeah. It happened that way with me and Casey and now it's happening again . . . with Brenda."

"Maybe you'll be luckier this time."

Wes started pacing. "Yeah, but maybe I won't. That's the hell of it. Something clicked between me and Brenda right away. She feels it, too. I know she does. But let's try to be rational here."

"Not an easy order," John said wryly.

Wes wasn't paying attention. "I don't have a great track record and neither does Brenda. The way she tells it, the two of you rushed into marriage same as me and Casey. We could both be making the same mistake twice." He shot John a look. "I shouldn't even be thinking about marriage at this point. I hardly know Brenda and already I'm thinking down the road to wedding bells." Wes stopped mid-step and pivoted round to face John. "I go gaga over a woman and right away I want to marry her, make babies with her . . ." He shook his head slowly. "I always wanted a family. I always pictured myself coming home to the little wife, three or four kids, the dog . . . maybe a cat or two . . . hell, maybe even chickens. Not in the house, of course."

"The wife and kids or the animals?"

"The chickens. Come on, John, you get the picture, don't you?"

John smiled briefly. "It's in sharp focus."

Wes scowled. "Not for Casey. It was always fuzzy for her. Her head was in a different place."

"Her career."

Wes nodded. "She'd just gotten this promotion to head of acquisitions for Hammond when we decided to get married. The promotion was a big move up for her. She was thrilled. I was thrilled for her. Don't get me wrong. I've got nothing against a wife having a career."

"As long as she can also look after a few kids, dogs, cats and chickens."

Wes smiled sheepishly. "Yeah, it's asking a lot. Not that I wouldn't help. I told Casey after we decided to get married that I'd take a different assignment at the paper, get out of the travel department, do something that would keep me at home. She was the one who talked me out of making a switch. She thought that since she'd need at least a year or two to feel her way in her new position and that it would be so time-consuming, it would work out better if I wasn't around all the time. Then, down the road..." He sighed. "Well, we never got too far down that road. I guess we both knew it was never going to work. We took different forks in the road right from the start."

"It happens that way sometimes," John said philosophically.

"I know. I don't hold it against Casey. She's very special."

"I agree."

Wes cocked his head. "Casey may play the part of a tough businesswoman who can handle anything, but I know her. She's plenty vulnerable. She just puts on a good front." He frowned. "I'll tell you something, John. You've really thrown Casey for a loop. I've never seen her like this before."

"I don't think I can take all the credit. Our dynamic Japanese duo deserve some of the credit, too."

"I'm not talking business here. I'm talking about Casey's heart. You think I don't remember that special gleam in her eyes? You think I don't remember the flush in her cheeks after... well, you know what I'm talking about. Casey doesn't fool around. Everything is serious to her. She takes everything to heart. I don't want to see her getting hurt. Do you know where I'm coming from?"

John walked over to Wes and placed a hand on his shoulder. "I'm crazy about her, Wes." He thumped his chest. "It hit *me* just like that, too."

"She's no ordinary woman, John. She's got enormous potential." Wes eyed him earnestly. "Unmined potential. She just needs the right . . ."

"Miner?"

Wes grinned. "Yeah. I was a lousy miner. No patience. I wanted to shape Casey into something she just didn't want to be."

"I like her shape just the way it is," John said, and both men smiled.

"So, you're crazy about her."

John's smile deepened. "Absolutely nuts."

Wes gave him a hearty slap on the back. "Good. That takes a load off my mind." A shadow crossed his face. "Of course, there's still me and Brenda to worry about."

John slung a comradely arm around Wes's shoulder as they walked out of the bedroom together. "Not that Brenda and I ever had a specific discussion about the topic, but I'd be willing to wager she wouldn't have anything against chickens. I'll tell you what. You and Brenda ever do decide on chickens you can count on me to build the coop for you. A wedding present. I'll be a pro after I build that hut for Casey," he added with a wink.

"So, David, how did you and Brenda first meet?" Akiko asked.

"Fate brought us together," David murmured dramatically, smiling over at Brenda, who'd just arrived in the kitchen. "Wouldn't you say that, Brenda?"

"Fate. Definitely fate," Brenda said airily, pouring some coffee and then sitting down beside Akiko.

"Ah," David said with a disconsolate sigh, "the fickle finger of fate."

Brenda had to hold back a laugh. David was so busy playing Olivier that he had no idea he was a born comedic actor.

"A fickle finger?" Akiko asked, bemused.

Brenda couldn't stifle her laugh. She pressed her hand to her mouth. "Sorry."

Akiko giggled. "Oh, dear, that American gesture. I did not know it was called a fickle finger."

Brenda laughed harder. "No, no. That's not what David meant. It's just an expression for things not working out the way we expect."

"Oh, I see," Akiko said brightly.

David leaned forward at the table. "But I'm hoping my luck will change now."

Akiko smiled sympathetically. "What is meant to be will be. That is an American expression, yes?"

"Absolutely," Brenda said, eyes twinkling.

David rose and walked over behind Brenda. He put his hands on her shoulders, leaned over and placed a warm, wet kiss on her cheek. "I'm Irish, Brenda. I don't buy this 'what will be' stuff. Ya gotta fight for what ya want. And I want you," he said in a Bogart growl.

Poor Bogie would have rolled over in his grave.

"I CAN FEEL your tension, Casey."

Casey sat cross-legged on the floor, facing Toho, trying desperately to will herself to relax. "I'm trying hard."

"That is the problem. You are trying too hard."

Casey closed her eyes. Too hard? If she'd been trying hard enough, she would never be in this mess right now. She wouldn't be feeling as though she were standing at the edge of a cliff with a row of people lined up behind her, any one of whom could push her off with one false move.

"You are thinking, Casey. You must make your mind blank."

Casey closed her eyes and tried to focus on the scent of incense filling the room, courtesy of Toho. The slightly pungent aroma only served to distract her further. She'd just as soon try some aikido again. At least that involved movement and activity, clumsy as she had felt beside the lean, athletic grace of Matoki.

Toho began a low rhythmic chant. Casey peered at him through hooded eyelids. He was sitting cross-legged like her, contentedly immobile; his head was bent, eyes closed, his expression serene, his breathing deep and even, his body in a state of complete relaxation. The chanting stopped after a few minutes, but Toho's position didn't change. Casey wondered if he hadn't fallen asleep, and she rested, opening her eyes wider, observing him speculatively.

She was struck by Toho's sharp, intelligent features, even with his face in a pose of deep relaxation. She was also struck by his ability to be so consistently strong and in control. Once upon a time she would have found herself identifying with Matoki. Now she found herself envying him.

Toho's gleaming black eyes flickered open, catching Casey's scrutiny. Casey flushed.

"Ah, Westerners." His voice was gently reproving, but then his lips curved in a faint smile. "You are all so individualistic. Really, you fascinate me. You and John, your brother, Brenda and Wes. All of you." He leaned a little closer. "But you, Casey, fascinate me most of all."

Casey smiled weakly. "Me?"

Toho rose to his feet with catlike athletic skill. He stood above her, looking down. "Being Japanese I would say the heart obstructs the mind. But perhaps that is not always true. In your case, I think the heart expands the mind."

Casey wasn't sure whether Toho saw that as a plus or not. Before she devised a subtle inquiry, the front doorbell rang.

Casey was just getting to her feet. The sound of the bell went through her like five-alarm chili. "Oh, no," she muttered under her breath, feeling rooted to the spot. "If that's another husband I give up."

"I beg your pardon, Casey?"

"Oh, nothing. I was just wondering if that was the...grocery boy...Henry. From the market." She gave a quick, nervous smile as she made her way jerkily to the door of the den. "I'll...go...see who it is. Why don't you just stay here and do some more...chanting?"

Casey did some silent chanting of her own as she headed apprehensively for the front door.

9

Tidings of comfort and joy...

"GOOD MORNING, Ms Croyden."

Casey froze. "Sheriff Mills. What... are you doing here? I thought you retired. And moved to Florida."

The sheriff, a tall, burly man with salt and pepper hair, partially covered by a wide-brimmed police-issue Stetson, gave Casey a broad smile. "I thought so, too. Then the new sheriff up and quit. Went off to Baltimore or some such place. I was back here visiting—somehow I just couldn't get used to all that sun and sand down South. So, here I am again, fillin' in till the town vote come January."

"I see," Casey said faintly.

He tipped his hat. "Going round to all the houses this side of the bridge to make sure everyone survived the nor'easter."

"Oh, yes, we're fine, just fine, thanks. No problem here. Nice of you to stop by and check on us. Nice to see you, too." Casey inched the door closed a little more with each word.

The sheriff, not budging, wiped his brow with the back of his gloved hand. "This here's the last house on my rounds. Mind if I come in to use your phone, Ms Croyden? Got trouble with the squawker in the cruiser, and I want to let the desk know that everyone down Ryder Road is A-okay."

One side of Casey's mouth turned down in a funny smile. Of all the people—next to another "husband"—that Casey didn't want to see at her door, Sheriff Mills had to rank first. He was one of the few people in the town who knew her personally. And more to the point, who knew Wes. They'd met last spring when Wes had come up to the house and discovered it had been vandalized. He'd called the sheriff, and in the process of tracking down the culprits, the two men had gotten chummy. When Casey arrived on the scene a few days later, she and Wes took the sheriff out for dinner to celebrate his upcoming retirement and move to Florida. Two weeks later she and Wes separated.

"I'm not actually sure my phone is working Sheriff."

"Why don't we give it a try? If it is out, you'll want to know so's we can get a repair man over for you. And, if it isn't asking too much, I'd sure appreciate a cup of coffee. Instant will do. It's mighty cold out. And the heater in the cruiser is acting up again. What do you expect, though? The car's five years old. You'd think the town would spring for a new one. Anyway, a nice hot cup of coffee would really hit the spot. If it's no trouble."

"Well . . . no. It's no trouble," Casey said reluctantly. Then she added eagerly, "I can even make you up a thermos to go. That is, if you're in a hurry. You must have lots to do. Cars stranded and all."

The sheriff chuckled. "Looks like you got a couple of cars badly in need of digging out. Tell you what. After the coffee, I'll pitch in and we'll get you mobile again. Now that the roads are being plowed and the bridge is open again, you might want to get into town." He peered over her shoulder and gave a little nod. If your, uh, masseur, can lend a hand, we'll have you dug out in no time."

"My . . . masseur?"

The sheriff gave another little nod, and Casey looked over her shoulder to see Toho in his white kung-fu-style outfit, standing in the hallway outside the den. Her "masseur" gave a formal bow, his expression solemn. If he was insulted by the sheriff's error, he gave no hint of it.

Casey's expression, on the other hand, was vivid with mortification. "Oh . . . oh, no. This is Mr. Matoki. My guest. My very special guest from Japan," she gasped.

The sheriff gave a little chuckle. "Sorry there, Mr. Matoki. Guess it was the native costume that fooled me," he said, nonplussed, removing his Stetson and scraping his boots on the mat.

"Please," Toho said pleasantly, "do not let it concern you. A very amusing mistake. It shall be one of the many delightful episodes I shall bring home to tell my family," he added as he walked over to the sheriff, who stepped into the hall, pulled off his gloves and stuck his meaty hand out for a handshake. First Matoki did another formal bow, the sheriff doing his best to mimic the greeting and shake Toho's hand at the same time.

Meanwhile, Casey closed the door with resignation, imagining the endlessly bizarre tales the hotel magnate would have to tell when he got home.

"Yeah, you can tell them back home about how you got snowed in during a real nor'easter, Mr. Matoki. Holed up for two whole days. I bet you've got a few funny stories to tell." The sheriff rubbed his icy hands together and then blew on them.

"Shall I ask Akiko to make a fresh pot of coffee for the sheriff, Casey?" Toho asked amiably.

"Oh, she doesn't have to bother," Casey said quickly, despairing of all the time fresh brewed would take and how long that would delay the garrulous sheriff's departure. Only when she saw that both men were giving her funny looks did she realize how rude her comment must have sounded. "I mean . . . I'll make the coffee. Akiko's my guest."

"I am sorry," Toho said stiffly. "I did not mean to usurp your position as hostess, Casey."

Things were going from bad to worse. "No, no. I don't think that at all, Toho. I adore Akiko's coffee. And it's so nice of her to pitch right in. I want her to feel at home. I want you both to feel at home."

"Any old coffee's good enough for me," the sheriff interrupted. "Don't want to put anyone to any special bother. Whatever you got's gotta be better than that muck my deputy makes down at the station."

As Sheriff Mills spoke, he unzipped his police-issue navy parka and hung it, along with his hat, on the coat rack in the hall. "I don't know what Jessie puts into that brew, but I'll tell you, it is foul tasting. Not that I have the heart to say anything to the boy. He hates that—my calling him a boy. He's close to thirty. But at sixty-three, he's a boy to me. Anyway, now and then I try to get down to the station ahead of him so's I can put up a halfways decent pot, but Jessie is an early riser. Most of the time he's down there at the crack of dawn, going over the police photos they send up from Concord, hoping to nab him a big-time bad guy. Not that we've had one of them criminals passing this way far as we know. No, this is a real sleepy little town. Not much in the way of crime around here. Oh, a couple of minor disturbances a year. Teens mostly. Getting their hands on a few six-packs and then kickin' up their heels. Specially round prom time."

The sheriff gave a little chuckle. "Like late last spring, remember, Ms Croyden?"

Casey, who was trying to figure out how she was going to keep the loquacious sheriff from running into Wes, running into her new "husband" John and running off at the mouth, didn't hear the sheriff's question.

Thinking she'd taken it rhetorically, he went on. "The McQuad boys and Tommy Ingram from down the other end of town broke in here last spring and smashed a couple of windows and spray painted the bathroom."

"It happens," Casey mumbled.

The sheriff was quick to assure Toho that the boys were soon captured. "Had myself a good assistant in tracking those hellions down," the sheriff went on. "Casey's husband had come up to open the house, and by the time he'd called me to report the break-in, he'd already gathered quite a few clues. He had a real nose for detective work, he did. Told him he ought to run for sheriff if he ever decided to quit his job with—"

"Sheriff," Casey jumped in, "hadn't you better call your deputy to let him know everything's fine? All of us . . . on Ryder Road?" Try as she might to hide it, her voice smacked of desperation, and both men gave her a curious look. Her effort to camouflage the effect with a bright smile only increased their bemused expressions.

The sheriff gave a little snort. "I know. I do go on sometimes. My wife, Jeannie, says I can talk a person's ear off." He glanced over at the telephone table near the staircase. "I'll just use your hall phone over there, Ms Croyden, if that's all right," Sheriff Mills said, bending down to take off his boots.

Casey nodded enthusiastically. Good, she thought. While he was on the phone, she could check on Wes and John. If they'd gone down to the kitchen, she'd keep them in there and give the sheriff his coffee in the living room. If her two "husbands" were still upstairs, she'd have time to race up the back stairs and tell them to stay put until she gave the all clear.

Having a plan made Casey feel a little less frantic. She was just going to say it was fine for the sheriff to use the hall phone when, out of the corner of her eye, she caught a glimpse of Wes and John descending the stairs.

That staircase was turning into nightmare alley. Casey saw her entire career slide past her eyes, a definite downhill slide. The sheriff was still bent over, working on a jammed zipper of his boot, when Casey made a lunging grab for his arm. In an inordinately loud voice, as if the sheriff had suddenly gone deaf, she shouted, "Oh, use the kitchen phone, Sheriff Mills. It's so much warmer in the kitchen. Don't worry about your boots. leave them on. A little snow won't hurt the floor."

"Hold on, hold on," the sheriff said, fighting Casey's efforts to uproot him. "I've got the zipper. There," he said, pulling off his boots and looking up at Casey with a satisfied smile.

His smile widened as he caught sight of the two men who had failed to make a hasty enough retreat back up the stairs.

"Well, hello there—"

Before the sheriff could call out Wes's name, Casey jumped in with "Look who's here, darling. It's Sheriff Mills."

Both Wes and John did a slow-motion about-face, matching smiles plastered on their mouths. They waved in unison from the top of the stairs.

The sheriff gave a wave back and then beamed at Casey. "Well, now, I guess the rumors I heard were all wrong. Some folks around here been sayin' you two got divorced."

Casey could feel Matoki's shrewd eyes boring into her. "Divorced?" Her heart descended to her stomach. "Who? Us? No. We're still . . . happily married." She gave a wan smile.

John swung an arm around Wes. "Yup, still happily married," he said with a perfect touch of ambiguity. The sheriff walked in his stocking feet to the bottom of the steps. "So, how's it going . . . ?"

Again Casey leaped in. "Wes, John, did the two of you . . . finish what you . . . had to do . . . upstairs?"

Before the men could respond, the sheriff, not one to be interrupted, motioned for Wes to come down. "Have a cup of coffee with me and tell me all about your trip to Tahiti. That was where you were heading when I saw you last spring, wasn't it?"

Casey's heart moved from her stomach to her feet.

Wes, not known for his quick thinking even in the best of times, muttered, "Oh . . . Tahiti."

It was John who, once again, came to Casey's rescue. "Ah, Tahiti" he said reflectively. "What a time we had in Tahiti, Wes and I. A great trip. Never saw a more beautiful spot. You ever get a chance, Sheriff, you really ought to go. A tropical paradise. Wouldn't you say so, Wes?"

"Yeah, yeah, definitely. Great spot."

"We could talk your ear off about Tahiti, right, Wes?" John went on amiably.

"Right," Wes said, making an attempt to pick up the ball.

"But—" John gave Wes a friendly slap on the shoulder "—Wes and I really do have to finish up a project we're working on. A design for a shed Casey wants built." John turned to Wes. "If we get a chance, we should go into town, buy the sheriff a beer and shoot the breeze."

Wes, not wanting to make a mistake, stuck to a silent nod.

Casey's eyes locked with John's for a brief moment. She had to fight the urge to go bounding up the stairs, throw her arms around him and cover his face with grateful kisses. She adored the man. She'd never have another squabble with him again. She was beaming, her smile spontaneous for the first time in days.

The smile didn't last very long.

"The shed? Ah, yes. I would very much like to see your design," Toho said. "Would you mind if I join you?"

Casey saw the blank look on Wes's face, but John once again came through. "Sure, come on up, Toho. We've scrapped a half-dozen plans. Maybe you have some suggestions. How about it, Wes? We'll begin with a clean slate."

Casey's smile reappeared, brighter than before. This was working out better than she could have hoped. With Toho safely tucked away upstairs she didn't have to worry about the sheriff getting into a discussion with him about her husband, Wes.

Casey forgot there was still Akiko to attend to, but her memory was quickly jogged by her petite guest's arrival.

Akiko joined the group and bowed slightly. Casey introduced her to the sheriff before he asked if she was Casey's new housekeeper. Then she looped her arm through his. "Let's go in the kitchen, Sheriff. You can make your call there, and I'll get you that cup of coffee."

Again Akiko bowed. "Brenda and I have made true New England corn muffins from *The Joy of Cooking* recipe book. Enough for all."

"Corn muffins happen to be my favorite." The sheriff's eyes sparkled. "This must be my lucky day."

Casey forced a withered smile.

Akiko was delighted. "Yes, very good muffins." She beamed at Casey. Your brother says, next to the ones your mother used to make, they are the best he has ever had."

"Brother?" Sheriff Mills echoed, mystified. "I didn't think . . ."

"You never met David, did you, Sheriff?" Casey said hurriedly. "I'm sure I've told you about him. He lives in Philadelphia. Well, maybe I never did mention him. Mmmm, those muffins smell fabulous, Akiko. Butter and jam on yours, Sheriff?" she asked as she led him off to the kitchen, Akiko following close behind, much to Casey's dismay.

Given the way her own luck was going, Casey wasn't surprised to find brother, David, still in the kitchen, munching away on muffins. Best corn muffins other than the ones their dear old mom used to bake. Casey had to smile for all her misery. If there was one thing her mother had an aversion to, it was baking.

Brenda was sitting beside David, finishing a cup of coffee. she gave Casey a questioning grimace after a glance at the new arrival.

"Meet Sheriff Mills," Casey announced. "Sheriff, my brother, David and my friend, Brenda."

David stood up to shake the sheriff's hand.

Brenda smiled coyly. "I hope you haven't come to arrest anyone, Sheriff."

Mills got a good chuckle out of that. "My cardinal rule is never cuff the hand that feeds you. I heard there were some mighty delicious corn muffins fresh out of the oven."

"Coming right up. Oh, and the phone is over by the door," Casey said, pointing to the wall phone.

The sheriff ambled over in his stocking feet and dialed his office.

"Hi, there, Jess. It's Ned. Calling from Ms Croyden's place. Car radio's on the blink again, but what else is new. Everything checks out down this way. The plows could put some stew on, though. Some of the back roads are still impassable. How're things in town?" After a brief pause, he said, "Good. Hold down the fort. I'll be back in about twenty minutes. Been invited for a muffin and coffee." Another pause. The sheriff chuckled. "I'll see what I can do." He looked over at Casey, who was pouring a cup of recently brewed coffee into a mug. "Wants to know if I could bring him back a muffin. Says he just made up a fresh pot of coffee to go with it." He raised his eyes to the ceiling as he said "coffee".

"Oh, plenty of muffins," Akiko offered.

The sheriff turned back to the receiver. "You're on, Jess. Yeah, I'll thank Ms Croyden. And her two pretty houseguests who baked them. One of them came all the way from Japan. She and her husband."

After a short pause, the sheriff put his hand over the mouthpiece and winked at Brenda. "Jess wants to know who the other pretty houseguest is. Told me if you're single to tell you to be sure to come to the Saint Denis Christmas dance. It's the night before Christmas Eve. Say, you all should come. It's quite a do." He turned his attention back to his deputy. "Ms Croyden's got a houseful of guests, so I was telling her to bring them all along. Oh, and Jessie, guess who else is here?" He gave Casey a broad wink.

Casey turned a sickly green. She had to think of something fast.

"Ms Croyden's husband—"

He was on the word "husband" when she let go of the mug of coffee in her hand, screaming even before the mug shattered on the quarry-tiled floor and the hot coffee splattered her trouser-clad legs.

Everyone, including the sheriff, who hung up abruptly on his deputy, rushed to Casey's aid.

"No, no, please, I'm fine," Casey said as they all dropped to their knees, vying for space to pull up her slacks and examine her legs for burns.

Wes, John and Toho, who'd heard Casey's scream all the way upstairs, came racing into the kitchen. With everyone kneeling at Casey's feet, the scene resembled some kind of bizarre ceremonial homage.

"Honestly, it's nothing," Casey insisted. "The coffee wasn't all that hot. It was more the shock than anything else."

"We'd better put some butter on it," Brenda said. "My mother always did that when I got burned."

"No," David said, "butter will only make the burn sizzle. Cool water. We should apply cool water."

"I've got a first-aid kit in the cruiser," the sheriff said. "Got some cream we can apply." He started to rise and then stopped. "Nope. Just remembered, we brought the kit into the station one day last week to treat a fellow with a bad gash. Ended up driving him over to the clinic cause he needed stitches...."

"Wait, I think there's some ointment in here," Wes said, walking over to a kitchen drawer. "Yeah, here it is."

Casey gave him a sharp look. How did an infrequent houseguest know where she kept such items?

Fortunately the Matokis were too busy offering their own advice on what to do for Casey to pay attention to Wes.

John, ever the take-charge guy, stepped in and took Casey's arm. "The first thing she should do is get out of those slacks. I've got some cortisone cream upstairs. You can use some of that." He was already guiding Casey out of the kitchen before the sheriff got to his feet.

"What was that all about?" John asked once they were out of earshot. "Are you hurt? Is it painful?"

Casey thrilled to the clear note of concern in his voice. "I'm fine. It's no more than a little surface burn. I was just about to hand the mug to the sheriff when he started to announce to his deputy that my husband *Wes* was here. I had to do something."

"That was a bloodcurdling scream. You scared the pants off me."

Casey's eyes impudently traveled the length of him.

John grinned. "Does this mean we're happily reunited in wedded bliss?"

They started up the stairs. "For such a brief union, it has been a pretty rocky marriage, hasn't it?"

"It's had its rocks and its soft spots," he murmured, cupping her face and placing a kiss laced with promise on her receptive lips.

She darted a quick look down the stairs, then threw her arms around John's neck. "I'd never be able to pull this off without you, John. And about the hotel deal . . ." She saw a shadow cross John's face. "Don't worry." she smiled. "I'm not going to suggest you be my assistant again. What I'd like to do is call Hammond himself and ask him to write you in on this deal fifty-fifty. With your business background and your knowledge of Japan, I'm sure Hammond would go for it. After we tie this deal up with a blue-and-pink ribbon, you might want to negotiate a more protracted arrangement with Hammond. He wants this deal badly. And if you helped me reel it in, you could write your own ticket with the company." Her eyes sparkled. "I know I intend to. I mean to turn this deal into a vice presidency for me."

The shadow didn't lift from John's face as they climbed to the top of the landing. Once there, he turned to Casey. "That's the bottom line, then."

Casey didn't understand. "You want more than a fifty-fifty split?"

"I mean the vice presidency. That's what this is all about."

Casey remained perplexed. "Of course that's what this is about. Do you think I'd go to these lengths if—" she stopped, a knowing look in her blue eyes. "Oh, that's where you're leading. You want to know where you and I stand."

"Things have happened pretty fast between us." He laughed dryly, then dramatized in a deep voice, " 'Faster than a speeding bullet, more powerful than a locomotive, able—' "

" 'To leap tall buildings in a single bound,' " Casey said, finishing the timeless introduction to *Superman* and grinned. "It's been all that. And more. And I don't regret a moment of it." Her grin broadened. "Well, I could have done without passing out cold in front of the Matokis."

"What I'm getting at, Casey, is . . ." He fixed her with a steady look. "It's been my style to put my work above everything else. I've been driven. But I've discovered that work isn't everything. That winning isn't everything. Do you understand what I'm saying?"

His tone was so intense Casey was taken aback. "I do understand."

"I never dreamed something like this . . . like you . . . would ever happen along. You've really got my head spinning."

"You're in good company." she paused, her eyes locking with his. "And whatever happens with the Matoki deal, win or lose, I feel like I've already won."

"You know what I'd really love for Christmas, darling?" He slid his arms around her, kissed her lightly and released her. "I'd love a promise of a New Year's kiss."

"That's a promise," Casey whispered.

"And to share a toast with you at the stroke of midnight, a toast to us, to our future. Is that rushing things too much, darling?" He gave her his best Gable leer.

She draped her arms around his neck. "No, John, no. I'm incredibly happy. Is it too greedy of me to imagine that I might have it all, everything I've ever hoped for?"

He gave a little laugh. "Win or lose—as long as you win, huh?"

"I never said it wouldn't be nice to win all around."

He smiled, but Casey thought it a sad smile.

"No," he whispered, "you didn't. Maybe we're both a little greedy in our own way."

He kissed her again, a bit more fiercely, pinning her against the landing wall. She let out a breathless laugh. "Here we are smooching, and down in the kitchen, Sheriff Mills thinks it's Wes and I who are happily reunited." Casey gasped as she realized the implications of what she was saying. "Oh, my goodness, where is my head? What have I done? I left Sheriff Mills in there with the Matokis." She started to spin around and head back downstairs, but John caught hold of her.

"Take it easy. Brenda, David and Wes will cover for you. You've got to change your slacks or the Matokis will think it's odd."

"Okay, but I'll change quickly. Please go back down and hold the fort. I'm not worried about Brenda being able to cover, but David and Wes..." She gave John a sardonic look that made him laugh.

"Yeah, I'd better look after those two." He gave her a quick but passionate kiss, patted her bottom, paused for a moment to watch her disappear into her bedroom—their bedroom—and then started down the stairs...only to lock eyes with Sheriff Mills... eyes that had clearly taken in the intimate little parting scene between him and Casey. There was nothing John could do but smile sheepishly at the sheriff as he came down the stairs.

Hearing the footsteps, Toho and Wes, who were several steps behind the sheriff, looked up.

"How's Casey?" Wes asked John amiably.

"Oh, fine," John muttered, feeling little daggers shooting from the sheriff's eyes. An image flitted through John's mind: Sheriff Mills throwing him up against the wall, slapping a pair of cuffs on him and hauling him off to jail. How long would a guy get in Vermont for hanky-panky with another man's supposed wife? Especially supposing the supposed husband was buddy-buddy with the local sheriff?

"I am so glad it was not a serious burn," Toho said, looking with a bemused glance from John to the sheriff.

It was apparent to John that Matoki picked up the tension. Not too much got by the canny hotel magnate.

Wes, oblivious to the shift in the air, smiled brightly. "I'm just seeing the sheriff to the door, and Toho's offered to go out to the cruiser and check out the sheriff's police radio that's on the blink. Wanna go along and learn from a master?"

"Please," Toho protested. "I have merely dabbled."

John would have liked nothing better than to escape the sheriff's glinty eyes. but he knew he couldn't leave

Toho and Mills alone out in the cruiser. "Sure," John said, "I'd love to learn from a master."

The sheriff, who had yet to remove his eyes from John, narrowed his gaze but didn't say a word. Then again, sometimes an expression could speak a thousand words.

"By the way, John," Wes said as John slipped on his jacket and boots, "the sheriff was nice enough to offer to help us shovel out the cars, but I told him we'd manage. Don't you agree?"

John nodded. "Oh, right. We'll manage."

"I bet you will," the sheriff muttered snidely, pulling on his boots.

Wes, who was right beside Mills, overheard the remark and gave the sheriff a befuddled look. Mills merely grunted as he slipped on his parka and donned his Stetson.

Toho and John started out the door, but the sheriff deliberately pretended trouble with the zipper of his boot.

"Can I give you a hand?" Wes asked, kneeling.

The sheriff took a firm hold of the hand Wes offered and looked the travel journalist square in the eyes. "Listen, Wes, if I were you I'd keep a close eye on your pal John and on the woman you love, if you get my drift."

Wes replied immediately, without thinking, "Oh, no, Sheriff. You're wrong about John and Brenda. There's nothing between them anymore. Nothing at all."

Now it was the sheriff's turn to look utterly baffled. "Brenda? You and Brenda?" His eyes trailed to the stairs, where Casey, in a dry pair of slacks, was bounding down the steps. The sheriff watched her descent and nodded slowly. "No wonder."

10

Don we now our gay apparel . . .

"WHAT A CHARMING tradition, Casey," Akiko said with delight as the whole group walked down Main street. All of the store fronts were decorated in Victorian Christmas motifs, the shopkeepers dressed in formal pinstriped suits and bustled gowns trimmed with velvet, satin and lace. Victorian-costumed carolers strolled the street, and jugglers and jesters followed along. At the far end of the closed-off thoroughfare, a large group of bundled-up children and their parents laughed uproariously at a Punch and Judy show.

A horse-drawn sleigh loaded with bundled-up holiday passengers circled merrily around the perimeter of the town common, moving to the syncopated rhythm of "Jingle Bells," which drifted out from large speakers strung up on the bandstand. Children frolicked in the snow, dogs scampered and barked, shoppers hurried about doing their last-minute shopping.

The day was clear and crisp, the air redolent with the scent of pine. Inside the shops there was the delightfully fragrant aroma of frankincense and myrrh. It was a scene straight out of a Currier and Ives print and the town tradition for years.

Toho Matoki, walking a bit ahead of Casey and the others, stopped at a storefront electronics display, but it was the tiny mechanical Santa and his elves gleefully at work making toys in Santa's shop that caught his eye. Akiko came and stood beside him, slipping her hand in his. The others, Casey, John, Wes, Brenda and David, stood behind the pair, all watching the eye-catching miniature show.

"Someday we will bring our grandchildren from Japan to experience a New England Christmas," Akiko said softly.

Toho smiled wistfully. "You are ever optimistic, my honorable consort, that our children will bestow us with such blessings," he replied, his tone teasing but tender.

Wes smiled at Brenda. "I'd like to walk my kids down this street someday."

Brenda touched Wes's cheek with her gloved hand. "So would I," she said.

David, standing on the other side of Brenda, stared sullenly at the display. "So would I," he repeated with mock despair.

Casey caught John's eye and suppressed her smile. Over the past week, David had put so much effort into his role of unrequited lover that Casey was beginning to wonder if he hadn't actually fallen under Brenda's spell. There was no finding out from the source, since David had insisted on staying in character whether or not the Matokis were around. Casey was sure Stanislavski would approve, but her "brother's" behavior was driving her a bit nutty.

Not that Casey was complaining. Since that near disaster almost a week ago when Sheriff Mills had arrived on her doorstep, life had gone miraculously smoothly for her. Even though she had gathered all her strength to prepare for the next impending disaster, amazingly, nothing had occurred. Her "family" and friends had settled into a comfortable routine. The mood around the old homestead was festive and relaxed. No more unexpected visitors—or, more pointedly, husbands—arrived on Casey's doorstep, no one in the household made a slip, and everyone got fully into the spirit of Christmas.

During the week, Casey taught Akiko and Toho to cross country ski, and they enjoyed festive morning treks through the snow. Brenda, Akiko and Casey baked holiday treats and made additional tree ornaments out of dough and papier mâché. John, Wes and Toho came up with a detailed blueprint for a new shed—Casey was actually thinking she might have it built. It was a beauty. And David made himself useful splitting wood for the fireplace and regaling one and all with amusing little tales of growing up—he and his kid sister, Casey, mom and dad, their dog Zonkers. David's stories were so engaging and delightful, Casey found herself wistfully thinking it would have been nice if they were true.

In the evenings Casey and her guests all sat around the fireplace in the living room, roasting marshmallows or chestnuts, chatting and playing parlor games. Toho and Akiko had never played charades before, but they were quick studies. Later, everyone would sing Christmas carols to David's piano accompaniment. As it turned out, her "brother" could play up a storm.

As Casey stood with the others on Main Street, looking at the charming window display of Santa and his busy elves, she realized she could not remember a time when she'd felt so relaxed, so happy, so brimming with good cheer. Toho had bolstered her spirits by showing increasing interest in her concept for his new hotel project. Although he remained noncommittal, she was convinced it was in the bag.

And even though John remained adamant about not wanting in on the Hammond-Matoki deal, he continued to offer ideas and suggestions for the project that only added to Toho's enthusiastic interest.

The days with her newfound family and friends were wonderful for Casey. But the times alone with John behind her closed bedroom door were best of all. Each night together held the charged excitement that Casey compared to Christmas morning—the anticipation, the intensity, the laughing, the sharing, the feeling that all was right with the world. It was as if she and John had invented romance, as if neither of them had ever experienced it before. And Casey hadn't. Not like this. With Wes there had been sparks, a brief flame, a heat that neither of them could sustain.

With John, Casey experienced a dazzling and endless array of fireworks. She never believed a love like this would come along. She felt enthralled, ecstatic and joyful. When she wasn't laughing delightedly, she found that she couldn't stop smiling. She smiled at John, at her "brother," at Wes and Brenda, at the Matokis, at the postman and the oil man. She was smiling now as she looked in on Santa and his busy elves in the charming window display.

Casey was so lost in her reverie, she didn't realize the rest of her party had left the shop window and were walking up the street again.

John, who'd remained at her side, tugged gently on the sleeve of her parka. "Where are you?" he whispered.

She raised her eyes and gave him a dreamy look. "I was snuggled in bed under my warm downy quilt, being caressed, stroked, made love to by the man of my dreams." Her blue eyes shone, her ever-present smile decidedly sultry. "Or was I in heaven?"

John pressed his hand to her rosy cheek. He'd been entranced by Casey from the start, but he never found her more beautiful and alluring than he did at that moment. There was something so tender about her expression just then that it quite took his breath away.

His chilled lips skimmed hers, her misty breath escaping as her lips parted and she kissed him back with enticing ardor.

"Let's ditch the rest of the party, and slip off to the local inn," he whispered in his best Gable baritone against her mouth.

Casey tilted her head back and offered up a regretful sigh. "I'm afraid it's you I have to ditch, darling. I can't very well buy your surprise present with you around."

He smiled slyly. "Give me my present early. In a cosy bedroom at the inn. Or should I say, in heaven?"

"Tempting, very tempting. But how would you feel on Christmas morn without a gift to open from me? And what would the Matokis think of a wife thoughtless enough to overlook a gift for her treasured husband?"

Casey picked up the slight tightening in John's facial muscles. She knew that it continued to bother him that this deal with Matoki was always at the edge of her thoughts even when they were talking about their personal relationship.

Casey kissed him again, fierce and passionate, ignoring the surprised but mostly amused stares of holiday passersby. She persisted until she felt him respond. And then, before the response got too strong on both their parts, she pulled away breathlessly. "Now," she murmured, "you can be on your own for a bit in case you have some private shopping to do."

John cocked his head. "Is that a hint?"

She gave him a coy look. "I hope I wasn't too subtle."

He grinned and put his arms around her. "Subtlety isn't your strong suit, thank heavens."

She hugged him tight, wanting to freeze the moment, wanting never to lose this feeling of joy.

When she loosened her grip, John didn't release her. "How can I let you go?" he whispered.

She tilted her head up, her eyes meeting his. She was surprised by the look of intensity she saw. "I don't want you to let me go."

The intensity in his eyes increased. It was in his voice, too, as he murmured her name.

His look disturbed her. There was nothing playful in it. Their brief but torrid relationship had always had an element of playfulness. Casey loved that. Until she'd begun this whole zany ruse, her life had been so structured and serious. Next to making love with John, she loved laughing with him, she loved his teasing wit.

"What is it, John?" she asked, a touch of panic in her voice. She began to regret her not so subtle hint that he go off and buy her something. Did John think she meant something like an engagement ring? Did he think she was rushing him?

But then she thought, wasn't John the one who wanted to toast to their future? Was he getting cold feet? Was he having second thoughts? Was she supposed to let him off the hook?

Before she could come up with any answers, she heard Brenda calling to her from outside a boutique a few shop doors down.

"Hey, Casey, let's pick out something positively extravagant for the dance tonight. Take a look in this window. There's a gown that's got your name on it "

Casey waved at Brenda. "Go on. I'll meet you inside." She quickly turned back to John, who gave her a distracted smile.

"What's wrong?" she asked anxiously. "Did I say something...?"

"No..."

"Do something...?"

"No..."

"Are you scared?"

"Scared?"

"About us?"

He blew on his hands. "There's something we need to talk about, Casey."

"Okay." She steeled herself.

His smile was softer, more tender. "Not now."

"When?"

"After Christmas. After the Matokis leave." He gave a little sigh. "After we stop our exercise in method acting."

"It isn't all an act, John. Not for me."

He leaned into her and kissed her lightly. "Not for me, either."

Somehow his words didn't comfort her. That "but" still hung in the air.

"Go ahead." He gave her a light, affectionate pat on her down-padded bottom. "Buy that gown with your name on it. And do the rest of your shopping."

Casey hesitated, her eyes remaining on John, but he had turned his attention back to the Christmas display in the window.

A little shiver ran through her as she reluctantly walked away. But she hadn't taken four steps before John called her name. She spun around, her expression edgy and nervous.

He was giving her his dazzling Gable grin. "Someday I'd like to bring our kids down this street on Christmas."

Our kids. He'd said "our kids." Casey blinked back tears as she gave him a megawatt smile. What a perfect Christmas. What an absolutely perfect Christmas this was turning out to be.

AS THE THREE WOMEN glided down the stairs in their holiday finery, the men, dressed in their Sunday best, stared up at them agog. For the gala Christmas dance at Saint Denis's Church tonight, Casey, Brenda and Akiko had decided to dress up as Victorian ladies, their ball-gowns purchased that afternoon in a quaint boutique in town that specialized in period clothes. The petite, delicate Akiko had selected a simple black velvet gown trimmed at the square-cut neck and puffed sleeves with creamy white lace, a lovely match with her ebony hair and flawless porcelain skin. Brenda looked alluringly coquettish in a crimson satin gown trimmed with tiny pearl buttons from neck to bodice, her chestnut hair piled high on her head with little tendrils falling loosely about her face. And Casey, forgoing the pink silk number that Brenda had thought had her name written on it, had opted for a stunning midnight-blue velvet gown that fell sultrily off her shoulders in many tucks and cascades of lace and ribbons. The bodice clung tightly and flounces accentuated her slender waist.

John started to applaud and the others joined in as the women floated down the stairs. After the men rained compliments on them all, Wes took Brenda's hand and told her she looked dazzling, while David scooted off to get her coat, his hands lingering on her shoulders after he helped her on with it. Toho's smile was filled with pride and affection for Akiko. He whispered something in her ear that made her giggle, her hand covering her mouth in embarrassed delight.

John held Casey back near the stairs as the others headed for the front door.

He caught her hands. "Wait. I bought you something."

"But it isn't Christmas yet."

"Can't a husband give his wife a gift before Christmas? Turn around and close your eyes."

A moment later, Casey gasped as she felt the band of velvet circle her neck. She opened her eyes and looked in the hall mirror at the delicate cameo fitted to a midnight-blue velvet ribbon.

"The cameo is beautiful. But how did you know the color of the band would match my dress so perfectly?"

"A little elf told me."

John's palms rested lightly on her smooth, creamy shoulders as he studied her reflection through the mirror. "You look incredibly beautiful tonight. There's magic in your eyes, Casey. I'd like to devour you on the spot."

Casey turned around to face him, her eyes sparkling. "I declare, my love, you take my breath away!"

"You ain't seen nothing yet," he whispered against her ear, his breath sending an erotic ripple down her spine.

John was right. As she joined Brenda and Akiko by the front door, the four men exchanged devilish smiles and abruptly disappeared into the den. A minute later they returned to the hall—transformed into four very dapper Victorian gentlemen in sweeping black capes and black satin top hats. They had to have hit the same antique clothing shop that afternoon.

Now it was the women's turn to applaud their handsome, debonair escorts. But the top hats and capes were only the start of what promised to be a wondrous evening.

A soft dingling sound from outside drew the women's attention from their dashing escorts.

"What's that?" Casey asked, starting for the door. John rushed forward and got there ahead of her, blocking her way.

"Are we all ready?" He addressed the whole group as he slipped Casey's hand in the crook of his arm. The others followed suit, Brenda sharing Wes's arm on one side and David's on the other. Only after all four men nodded and winked did John open the door.

Outside, a light snow was falling like diamond dust, a beautiful sight. But it was the horse-drawn sleigh pulled up to the drive that made all three women gasp with delight.

Casey's eyes shot up to John. "That's the sleigh that was going round the green today. But how did you—"

He lowered his lips to hers and caught them opened in surprise. She flung her arms round his neck and kissed him back with delight.

Everyone snuggled under the heavy wool blankets in the open sleigh, David sitting up front with the driver. To the sound of sleigh bells ringing, they rode to the Saint Denis Church in town.

THE DANCE WAS WELL under way when they arrived. Admiring eyes turned as the elegantly costumed group entered the large reception room behind the church.

The organizers of the dance had done themselves proud. The room was festooned with tinsel, swirls of red and green crepe paper and strings of multicolored lights. Pine swags looped their way up the support columns. The tables ringing the hall were brightened with shiny red plastic covers. Red candles springing from freshly cut holly branches served as centerpieces. Groups of men and women gathered at the buffet tables to sample the array of sliced meats, three-bean salad, baked beans, sweet-and-sour meatballs, cakes and holiday cookies. Another group hovered around the enormous punch bowl filled with egg nog.

In the center of the room, a few couples danced dreamily to the melodious strains of the town's four-man band, the Dorset Warblers, while giddy, giggling tiny tots weaved in and out among the crowd.

After Casey's group claimed a table, John escorted her to the dance floor. Out of the corner of her eye, Casey caught the disapproving glance of Sheriff Mills, who was already on the dance floor, doing an awkward imitation of a waltz with his wife, Jeannie. Casey saw the sheriff bend low and whisper something in his wife's ear and the gray-haired woman immediately shot Casey and John a reproving look.

"Uh-oh, I'd better make sure I dance a couple of dances with Wes tonight, for the sheriff's sake," Casey murmured to John as he took her in his arms.

"Don't worry about it. Small towns thrive on this kind of gossip." John entwined his fingers behind Casey's back, swiveling slowly back and forth with her to the music.

Casey lifted the hem of her full skirt, holding it out like an open fan as she let John guide her about the dance floor. She pressed her cheek to his, and as he swirled her gracefully around she forgot about the sheriff and everything but the enthralling man holding her in his arms.

"You're a wonderful dancer," Casey said dreamily. "You do everything wonderfully."

"You bring out the best in me, darling," John replied, dipping her low, holding her poised, then slowly lifting her.

Brenda and Wes were dancing nearby.

"Hey, what gives with the sheriff tonight?" Brenda asked Casey. "I said hello and he gave me a dirty look."

Casey grinned. "I have a feeling he thinks you're fooling around with my husband."

Wes pulled Brenda closer. "What a great idea."

As the next dance began, John did a switch with Wes, whisking Brenda off for a fox-trot. As Wes began dancing with Casey, he kept glancing over at the divorced couple. Casey glanced over, too. John was holding Brenda close, his lips pressed against her ear. He was saying something to her as they danced that brought a concerned look to Brenda's face. She tilted her head back. Now she was saying something to John that made him scowl.

"What's that all about?" Wes muttered.

"They still have some business to settle," Casey replied. "That's why they came up here in the first place."

"Business?"

"Financial stuff," she said distractedly, watching John and Brenda walk off the dance floor and head for a secluded corner, where they continued what looked to be an increasingly more heated conversation.

Wes, busy watching the interchange between John and Brenda, lost the beat and accidentally stepped on Casey's toe.

"Sorry." He frowned. "Oh, now Quinn is going over there. Damn, that guy can be a royal pain." He glanced down at Casey. "You don't think he's really interested in Brenda, do you, Case?"

"I don't know," She muttered, noticing that John was none too happy watching David whisk Brenda away for a dance. Casey's eyes met John's and they locked for a brief moment. He smiled at her, but the smile didn't reach his eyes. He looked disturbed. Something was wrong. Casey felt that same panicky sensation she'd felt that afternoon when John had said they had to talk. Talk about what? About the unfinished business between him and Brenda?

John asked Akiko to dance the next dance while Toho went to the buffet table to sample some New England fare. Wes cut in on David, putting a possessive arm around Brenda's waist, and Casey ended up dancing with David.

"What does she see in him, anyway?" David asked Casey.

"Wes is a very nice man."

"I'm not talking about Wes."

Casey suddenly felt like an elephant had just sat down on her chest. "You're not?"

"She's still in love with her ex-husband."

"What?"

"Come on, Casey. An actor has to be very intuitive. He picks up undercurrents—he's especially sensitive." He sighed wearily. "Besides, I caught the two of them in the kitchen the other day when they thought I was off cross-country skiing with the rest of you."

Casey's heart was pounding furiously. "Caught them?"

David shrugged. "They sprang apart when they heard me walk in. Man, I never saw a more guilty-looking twosome. Brenda was all flushed and John went as white as freshly fallen snow. No one knew what to say. Then

Brenda rushed out and I went after her, but she said she didn't want to talk about it."

"And . . . John?"

"He didn't look like he wanted to talk about it, either."

Casey stopped dancing. "I have a headache, David. Mind if we cut this short?"

He escorted her off the dance floor. "I'm sorry, Casey. For an actor, I wasn't being very sensitive just now. I mean—you and John . . ."

"Just letting the act get out of hand," she muttered.

Later that evening, dancing again with John, he looked sternly down at her. "What's the matter? Did the sheriff make some snide remark to you?"

"The sheriff?"

"Then what?"

"Nothing. Nothing's wrong," she said stiffly.

"I thought we didn't keep secrets from each other."

"Stop it, " she said sharply. "Let's stop the act."

"I have a better idea. Let's get out of here."

He led her off the dance floor as she tried to protest. "We can't . . ."

"Watch it, darling. You don't want Toho to think we're having another squabble." He was leading her over to their table for their wraps. The others were all there, sipping egg nogs. John scooped up his cape and Casey's coat.

"Casey and I are going to spend the night at the Dorset Inn across the road. We'll see you back at the house tomorrow," John announced, giving the group a broad wink.

"But . . . but, I can't do that," Casey protested. "I can't . . . we can't just leave our guests to fend for themselves."

John gave David a nod. "Your brother can play host for the night, darling."

"Do not worry, Casey," Akiko assured her. "We will be fine. You should be most thrilled to have such a romantic husband." She gave Toho a little nudge. "Remember that wonderful inn near the Bridge of Heaven on the Sea of Japan." A rosy hue colored her porcelain cheeks as she smiled demurely at the others. "Toho arranged it all. A package holiday called the Honeymooners' Romance Special. And us—an old married couple of twenty-seven years. Yes, it is never too late for romance."

Casey had no choice but to meekly follow John as he ushered her out of the church hall. But once they were outside, she proceeded to argue with him all the way across the road to the inn, the whole time John registered at the desk and all the way up to their room—the honeymoon suite, of all things.

She was stepping into the room, catching her breath for a second go around, when he leaned her up against the wall just inside the door.

"John . . ."

"I'm crazy about you, Casey."

"Let's talk."

His mouth made an erotic trail up her neck.

"About you . . . and . . . Brenda." She was breathless.

He was feasting on her earlobe. "Later."

She felt the zipper of her gown open. "Do you . . . still love her?"

He kissed her lips. The brief sensation made her feel woozy.

"John . . ." She felt her gown slide off her shoulders, down her legs. Her legs ached, her whole body throbbed.

"I never loved her, Casey. That's the truth."

She thrilled to his confession. "Oh, John..." She didn't finish. John's lips got in the way. She stepped out of her gown, first one foot, then the other.

Their kiss deepened, a wild crushing of tongue and lips, their mingled breath charged with an erotic current. His hands cupped her buttocks, the heat of his palms penetrating her thin silk panties. Casey's limbs felt heavy, languorous. There was a soft rustle of cloth.

John pinned her to the wall. Not ten feet away was a perfectly quaint and inviting four-poster.

Later, she thought dimly, as his mouth cruised down her body and she started to dissolve....

HER BODY FIT PERFECTLY to his as they stretched out on the four-poster. Like two matched pieces of a puzzle. John's hands stroked and caressed her, exploring the shape of her body, reveling in it. Casey was slender, but there was a womanliness about her, a fullness to her breasts and hips that John found deliciously appealing. His palms cupped her breasts.

"Beautiful," he whispered. "You're so beautiful." He put his lips to her nipple. She shivered, pressing harder into him, her lips parting.

"Do you like that?"

"Yes," she murmured. "Yes, that's wonderful. Oh."

His mouth, his lips, his tongue caressed her soft flesh, searching, primal. She could feel her muscles tighten as his tongue slid over her belly, followed the curve of her hip, glided between her legs, his hands coaxing them apart. She let out a little cry and tensed, an instinctive response to his erotic onslaught. But John's seduction was relentless and inspired. A heat spread through her limbs and Casey felt herself open to him. She emitted a soft, low sound like a hum, her face flushed with excitement and need. Shedding any vestige of inhibition, she locked her ankles at his waist and let the sensations sweep over her, rock her, envelop her.

While she still fought for breath, he sought her lips, kissing her deeply. He entered her in one smooth, swift slide. As John filled her, Casey cried out his name over and over, her hands against his back, kneading his spine, his buttocks. John shifted position and pulled her on top of him. She rose up over him, his hands gripping her waist, his bent knees supporting her spine as she arched back.

As they moved, they seemed to shed the boundaries of their bodies, melding into one their own unique rhythm hurling them closer and closer to fulfillment until finally, they came.

Outside it began to snow and the wind rattled the old windows of the inn. Casey lay snuggled in John's arms. He drew her close, warming her with his body, not bothering to reclaim the covers that had slipped off the bed while they'd made love.

She turned one her side so that she faced him. Quietly she studied him, then slowly traced the line of his strong profile with the tip of her finger.

"John?"

"Yes, darling?"

She hesitated. "Let's put the ghosts of Christmas past behind us once and for all."

He turned his head to meet her serious gaze. "Do you have any particular ghosts in mind?"

"David surprised you and Brenda in the kitchen the other morning. He seems to think that the two of you were..."

"We were discussing business, Casey, nothing more. If we looked surprised, we were. We thought you'd all gone. When David popped in we thought one of the Matokis might be with him, that we might have given our hand away. But, I swear to you, Casey, we were only going over some joint business holdings, trying to settle them."

"And have you? Settled them?"

His eyes flickered over her face. "Almost." He was quiet for a moment and then he said, "I want to settle my account with Brenda quickly, especially now."

"And is Brenda in agreement?"

There was a sardonic edge to his smile. "She's coming around."

He pulled Casey closer. "Now can we put the ghosts of Christmas past to rest? I much prefer to focus my attention on flesh and blood. Namely your flesh, my lovely."

Casey laughed, then responded with a deliciously wanton kiss.

As they began making love again, a wave of possessiveness gripped Casey. She truly felt at that moment that John was her husband. She had no legal right to the feeling, but there it was.

11

'Twas the "day" before Christmas and . . .

LATE THE NEXT MORNING, after an unbelievably romantic tryst at the Dorset Inn in the arms of the man she felt certain was the most wonderful, incredible, tender and endearing member of the male species ever to come along, Casey was walking on air. She was hearing love songs in her head. The sky looked bluer, the air smelled more fragrant, the snow was whiter than ever before.

When she heard the front doorbell ring, she was sitting cross-legged on the floor in the living room, wrapping some last-minute gifts. David, Wes, Brenda and Toho were playing bridge in the den and John and Akiko were chatting over hot chocolates in the kitchen after an invigorating cross-country ski run.

Casey felt a prickle of alarm at the shrill ring of the bell. After all, that sound had not exactly been the prelude to glad tidings up to now. But then she quickly ran through the possibilities. There really were no more husbands who could show up, no reason for Sheriff Mills to reappear, no one else she knew in town who would pop in for a visit.

I bet, she told herself naively, *someone's lost their way and needs directions*. Dropping the red ribbon she'd been about to tie in a festive bow Casey rose from the floor.

The doorbell rang again as Casey was stepping into the hall. David popped out of the den and glanced back at her, a clear look of concern on his face. "Should I get it?"

She gave him a confident nod.

Still, for all her confidence, Casey felt a little shiver shoot down her spine as David, after a brief hesitation, went to see who was there. She wasn't aware she was holding her breath until he actually opened the door. Then she heard the air in her lungs let go in a nervous whoosh.

"Jane. Oh . . . Jane." Casey had forgotten that her assistant was going to stop by on her way over to Ingram for the holidays, where her folks owned a weekend home. Furthermore, Casey had been so discombobulated all week she'd never thought to phone Jane and update her on all the last-minute changes to the original plan.

Jane, bundled up in a black down coat and black knit hat, extended an armload of brightly wrapped gifts to Casey. "To put under your tree. A little something for the Matokis and then a gift for you and . . ." Jane looked over at David, who was standing beside Casey, then gave Casey a broad wink. "For your husband."

"What? Nothing for the dear old bro?" David said sotto voce, returning the wink.

Jane scowled. "Bro?"

"Short for brother," David said in a whisper.

"But I thought—"

"It's a bit confusing," Casey broke in. And too complicated to consider going into at the moment, she decided. "Don't worry. I'll explain when we're back at work next week," she said abruptly, taking the presents from Jane's arms. "Thanks for stopping by. Be sure to give your folks my regards. Merry Christmas."

Casey was about to shut the door in the face of her be-fuddled assistant, when she heard a familiar baritone voice behind her.

"Well, well, darling, I didn't know we were expecting more company." John sauntered up the hall to the door and slung a possessive arm around Casey. "Akiko and I were wondering who it could be." He glanced over his shoulder. "Weren't we, Akiko?"

Jane was staring wide-eyed at John. "'Darling'" she said, blinking.

Casey plastered a bright smile on her dry lips. "Oh, Jane just stopped by for a minute," Casey said hurriedly. "To bring us some gifts."

"Why, thanks, Jane. That was really sweet of you," John said amiably, planting a light kiss on the cheek of Casey's startled assistant.

Jane looked over at Casey with a thoroughly bewildered expression.

"And you haven't met Akiko," Casey said quickly, to keep her assistant from asking any questions or saying the wrong thing, such as, "What's this about a brother, and what are you doing with the wrong husband?"

After a hasty introduction, Casey went on in a rush to say, "So, thanks again for the gifts, Jane. I know you're in a hurry to see your folks so we won't keep you. Give them my love and have a great Christmas."

Casey was once again about to close the front door on her perplexed assistant, when the rest of the bridge team—Brenda, Toho and Wes—popped out of the den. Casey glanced from them to Jane, not surprised to see her assistant's mouth drop open. Jane, of course, knew Wes. Poor Jane. Three husbands? Including one that was once legit? Jane had gone stark white. Casey worried that the poor woman might actually faint.

Casey gave Jane's arm a reassuring squeeze as she raced through more introductions, praying that her dazed assistant would simply keep her mouth shut. Casey wasn't too worried. Jane looked positively speechless.

However, her speech came back before Casey managed to get her on her way.

"I've got to talk to you," Jane croaked just as Casey was saying what she hoped would be a final farewell.

"If it's about work, don't worry. Everything's under control."

"No . . . really, Casey. It's important."

Casey knew she owed Jane an explanation, but she really wasn't up to it at the moment. "We'll go over everything when we get back to work."

But Jane's hand was forcefully holding the door, and Casey had no recourse but to step aside. "Okay, Jane. Sure. Come on in."

As Jane stepped into the hall, her eyes, wide as saucers, were riveted on Wes, who was standing there with his arm around Brenda. For his part, Wes wore a cheery smile. But Brenda, Casey noted, was taking a turn at looking rather pale. Maybe Brenda was nervous that Jane was an old love from Wes's past. She was certainly giving Jane a wary, keep off kind of look.

"Why don't we go in the den and have a little chat?" Casey suggested to Jane.

"Perhaps," Akiko said in a soft voice, "your assistant would first enjoy a warming cup of hot chocolate. John and I were just about to bring some into the living room for everyone."

"No . . . I . . ." Jane gave Casey a desperate look.

"And there are some very nice Christmas cookies," Akiko added.

Obliged to play the proper hostess, Casey was forced to forestall her private little tête-à-tête with her assistant. "Yes, come inside and have a hot drink, Jane. Then we'll talk." She looked down at the gifts in her arms. "I'll just put these under the tree, then I'll bring in a tray of drinks and cookies. Akiko and Brenda baked them. Brenda's recipe. They're wonderful."

Jane's gaze flew to Brenda.

Brenda smiled weakly.

John and Casey exchanged puzzled looks. So, behind them, did Toho and Akiko.

There was an awkward silence.

"Here, let me help you off with your coat," David said, stepping up to Jane.

She fumbled with the buttons. "Casey, I really do need . . ." But Casey was already heading into the living room to put Jane's gifts under the tree.

"So how were the roads coming up?" Wes broke in as David helped Jane off with her coat and plucked her hat from her head.

"The roads?" she mumbled, as David hung up her things and led her off in the direction of the living room.

"Mmmm. I bet they're still pretty bad." Wes's arm slipped off Brenda's shoulder and reached for her hand as they followed behind David and Jane. "Boy, Bren, your hands are like ice."

Casey was tucking the presents under the tree as the others came into the room. "Well," she said, rising, "I'll go get the cookies and—"

"Oh, no, let me," Brenda piped in. "You stay and chat with Jane." She looked over at John. "You know where everything is, John. Why don't you come and help me in the kitchen?"

Casey gave Brenda a grateful smile, acknowledging that Brenda was doing her best to subtly clarify for the befuddled Jane that John was the official "husband" of the moment.

"I'll help you, Bren," Wes offered, instead, swinging his arm back around her shoulder, giving Jane a crooked grin at the same time. "I'm trying to make amends. Bren and I had a big row back home over my not pitching in around the house. She stormed out and came up here to have a good cry on her old friend Casey's shoulder. I followed her and . . ."

"I think Jane gets the idea," Casey broke in, motioning to Wes to take Brenda and go get the hot chocolate and cookies.

Casey smiled encouragingly at Jane, who, to her surprise, didn't seem to be as quick on the uptake as she would have expected. David noticed that, too, so he decided it was time for him to come to the rescue.

"Jane, you know my sister. Quite the little matchmaker, Casey is."

"Poor David," John said with a faint smile. "You see, before Wes and Brenda were together, David and Brenda were seeing each other. When Brenda showed up here alone, vowing she and Wes were through, David kind of thought maybe he and Brenda could get something going again."

"That's the whole sad story," David said with a deep sigh.

Casey clapped her hands. "That about sums it up." She snuck a nervous glance at Akiko and Toho, who were sitting side by side on the sofa, observing the little drama with rapt interest.

During the few minutes that Wes and Brenda were off in the kitchen, David and John both put on admirable

performances that seemed wasted on Jane, who continued plying Casey with beseeching looks. Casey was
growing increasingly irritated by her assistant's dense
manner. Jane was usually so sharp.

When Wes and Brenda returned to the living room,
Casey began pouring hot chocolate into cups. She felt a
little like Alice in Wonderland presiding over the Mad
Hatter's tea party. John helped distribute the cups and
Akiko went around offering cookies.

Casey remained puzzled as to why Jane continued to
look so dazed. Hadn't Casey's brilliant ensemble of am-
ateur and professional actors provided enough clues to
give her a reasonably clear picture of what was going on?

"So how are things at the office?" Casey asked non-
chalantly, giving her assistant a reassuring smile.

Jane seemed to be having some difficulty digesting her
wreath-shaped sugar cookie. All she could manage was
a shrug.

Brenda, still looking decidedly pale, suddenly popped
up with the suggestion that everyone go cross-country
skiing.

"Akiko and I just came back from the trails, Brenda,"
John said, puzzled. "Anyway, you don't look too good."

"Yeah," Wes agreed. "Her hands are like ice." He took
one of her hands in his. "Why, you're trembling, Bren."

"I guess...I'm not feeling too well." She rose abruptly,
turning to John. "Maybe you've got some aspirin upstairs."

"Uh...sure," John said. But as he started to get up, Wes
popped up beside Brenda.

"That's okay, John. I've got something better than aspirin for Bren. Come on, babe. I'll fix you up."

Brenda sat back down. "No, no. I think it's passing."

"What is passing?" Toho asked, tossing a wild card into the pot.

"My... headache," Brenda said.

Akiko smiled sympathetically. "Oh, yes, my daughter suffers terrible headaches, as well. I believe it is stress. That is possible."

Jane gulped down her hot chocolate in record time. "Casey, I really do need to talk to you."

Casey nodded, eager to get the little chat over with and then dispatch Jane on her way to her parents. Ever since she'd shown up at the door, there'd been a new current of tension in the house. It was a wonder Casey didn't have a splitting headache.

"Well, if you'll excuse me and Jane for a few minutes... we really do have a bit of catching up to do." Casey rested her gaze on Toho. "Actually, Jane's arrival was quite provident. Now I can give her the additional notes on the proposal and—" she turned to Jane "—if you have time while you're up at your folks, maybe you can check it over, and then we'll fax it right off to Tokyo after the holiday."

"Yeah... sure," Jane muttered as she and Casey started out of the living room. They got as far as the doorway, when they heard a loud gasp and then the clatter of cups. Swinging around, the two women saw Brenda stretched out on the floor in a dead faint.

Wes carefully lifted Brenda in his arms and laid her out on the sofa. Casey ran to get some water, but by the time she got back, Brenda was coming to, with the others hovering around her.

"Give her some air," Casey suggested, pouring a glass of water from the pitcher for Brenda to sip on.

Akiko was kneeling beside Brenda, a gentle smile on her face as Casey came over with the glass. "Perhaps I was wrong about stress as the cause of your symptoms, Brenda."

Brenda looked a little dazed by Akiko's remark. "What . . . do you . . . mean?"

Akiko looked over at Wes, who was hovering closest to Brenda. "Perhaps this is not the first morning Brenda has had a headache and dizzy spell?"

A low moan escaped Casey's lips, and the glass of water in her hand clattered to the floor. For a brief moment, her eyes bore into John's. He slowly shook his head, his expression perplexed.

At first Brenda didn't get it. When she did, her eyes widened. "No...oh, no," Brenda protested. "I'm not...I couldn't be . . . pregnant." But immediately her eyes shot over to John.

Casey caught the look and fled from the room in tears.

"Casey. . ." Both John and Jane called out her name in unison, running after her.

Brenda called out to Casey, too, but as she started to rise from the couch Akiko insisted she stay put.

Brenda sighed, then looked over at Wes. He hesitated for a moment, then sat beside her and drew his arm around her. "It'll be okay, Bren. Honest it will. I'll marry you."

"Goes ditto for me, Brenda," David said in a sad, earnest voice.

Akiko looked over at Toho and smiled, then proceeded to meticulously clean up the mess of broken glass and porcelain cups that lay shattered on the floor.

Casey had fled upstairs to her bedroom, followed by Jane and John, who were vying angrily with each other for a chance to talk to Casey alone.

"Oh, go away both of you," Casey pleaded. The strain had finally gotten to her, the latest glitch in the scenario just to much to bear. Through it all, she'd believed in John, trusted him, bought his story that there was nothing between him and his ex-wife. With John on her side, she felt as if she could conquer the world, certainly win Toho Matoki over. And she had. Only now, it didn't even seem to matter. Nothing seemed to matter.

"Casey, you've got to believe me, Brenda's not pregnant," John insisted.

Even if Brenda wasn't pregnant, Casey would never forget the guilty look Brenda had shared with John.

"Look, whoever you are," Jane said in a low, seething voice, "can't you see how distraught Casey is? Now do what she says and just get out of here."

John eyeballed her defiantly. "She told us to both get out. Where do you come off . . . ?"

"Who the hell are you, anyway? How did you end up as Casey's husband?" Jane demanded.

"He's Brenda's husband." Casey sank down on her bed.

"Ex-husband," John shot back.

"Ex-husband?" Jane's eyes narrowed.

"Brenda isn't pregnant. Not by me, anyway." John looked beseechingly over at Casey. "You've got to believe me."

"I wouldn't believe a word this guy says," Jane warned.

Casey sighed. "You don't even know him." Then, realizing she was jumping to John's defense, she snapped, "But you've got good instincts."

"Casey, this is no time to fall apart." He walked over to the bed. "Are you forgetting the Matokis are downstairs? Are you forgetting all about your big dream of a vice presidency? Are you forgetting how much you've gone through to clinch this hotel deal? Come on, darling. You've got to pull yourself together for your own sake."

Jane strode over to the bed. "Casey, listen to me. This guy and Brenda—"

"Will you leave her alone. Can't you see how upset she is?"

"She had every right to be upset and you and Brenda know it," Jane snapped.

"I tell you, Brenda is not pregnant. I haven't slept with her." And then, after a brief pause, he added, "In ages."

"Stop it, both of you. I can't think straight," Casey protested.

There was a light rap on her bedroom door and Akiko's lilting voice drifted in. "Excuse me. John. Wes insists on taking Brenda to town to see the doctor, but his car is stuck in a snowdrift. Could you please come help?"

John stared at Casey. He seemed to be having a hard time pulling his thoughts together.

A second knock. "John, will you come?"

He gave Casey one last heartfelt look. "Yes, I'm coming."

Casey rolled over on her stomach and buried her head in the pillow as John left the room.

Jane sat down on the edge of the bed. "Oh, Casey, what have you done?"

Through muffled tears, she answered, "I've fallen in love . . . with the wrong husband."

"You can say that again," Jane said with such vehemence that Casey stopped crying and rolled over on her back. "And as for Brenda . . ."

"Brenda's been wonderful. You don't know the half of what's been going on here."

"It looks to me like you don't, either. John and Brenda . . ."

"They've both been great. All of them have. John, Brenda, David, Wes." Cutting off Jane's constant attempts to interrupt, Casey rehashed the whole zany sequence of events that had unfolded during the week. When she finally finished, Jane stared at her with a look that combined disbelief with pity.

"The bastards," she muttered, shaking her head. "Both of them."

Casey sighed wearily. "Poor Wes. He's in love with Brenda. I think David is a little bit in love with her, too."

"Oh, forget Wes and David, Casey. I'm afraid you've got bigger problems. You've been royally duped."

"I know that. Why do you think I'm so miserable? How will I ever pull myself together now to carry off the deal with Toho? Suddenly it doesn't even seem that important to me. Oh, God, I really am in love." She started to cry in earnest.

Jane took firm hold of Casey's shoulders and gave her a shake. "I mean it, Casey. You really don't know the half of it. Do you know who Brenda works for?"

Casey blinked. "For a law firm, I think."

"She works for the Kirkland Hotel group. I know."

Casey stared dumbly at her assistant.

"Remember, I used to work there, too. Before I came to Hammond. Brenda more than works there. She's the executive assistant to Kirkland himself." Jane hesitated. "John must work for Kirkland, as well. They must be in this together, a plot to steal the Matoki deal right out from under us."

"No," Casey said. "No, he can't . . . He wouldn't."

"Brenda recognized me, Casey. Why do you think she acted so strangely, looked so pale, tried to do everything she could to prevent us from having a private talk? Why do you think she kept giving John those desperate looks? If Brenda's pregnant, I'll eat the entire Matoki file. She just wanted to warn your darling ersatz husband that the jig was up."

Casey sat perfectly still, perfectly silent, her eyes fixed on Jane. She was dry-eyed now. No emotion at all showed on her face. But as she sat staring at her assistant, Casey distinctly heard her heart crack, like the sound of a pencil snapped in half.

After a long silence, Casey said without inflection, "I handed John the chance of a lifetime to get at Matoki." Her composed expression started to crumble.

"Oh, Casey, I'm sorry. Really I am."

"What I want to know is, how did John find out the Matokis were coming here?"

"Kirkland must have gotten to someone at our place. He knows your reputation. If anyone was going to get to Matoki, you stood the best chance. The question is, what are we going to do now?"

Casey remained silent and motionless. Jane began to worry she might have gone over the edge.

"We can't let them get away with it. We have to fight back. Come on, you're a fighter, Casey."

As Casey continued to stare at Jane, a fire began to blaze in her vivid blue eyes. "I was almost willing to forgive him an...indiscretion. I mean...he and Brenda...a moment of passion...a moment maybe he regretted." She blinked back tears. "Who am I kidding? I was probably willing to forgive him almost anything. *Almost* anything," she repeated, springing from the bed and launching into agitated pacing. "But this...this is taking it one step too far. Dirty underhanded business dealing. Oh, no. No way. Not with this cookie. Nobody pulls a deal out from under Casey Croyden's nose. Nobody gets the chance to laugh out the other side of his face on my account. If anybody is going to get the last laugh on this deal, it's going to be me. Even if I have to die laughing."

Jane perked up. "Okay, now you're talking. Now the old Casey's back. So what do we do?"

Casey swung around and gripped Jane's hands. "What we've got to do is get Toho to sign on the dotted line before he leaves. John is banking on the fact that Toho won't make any decision until after the holidays. He and Brenda have probably been secretly putting together their proposal and will zip it off to Toho under the Kirkland banner as soon as Christmas is over."

"I'm sure of it," Jane said.

Casey started pacing again. "The things that man said. New Year's Eve. Toasting our future." She came to a stop, crossed her arms over her chest and hugged herself. "How could I have been such a fool?"

"Don't blame yourself, Casey. He is . . . very good-looking. Kind of reminds me of Clark Gable. . . ."

"Don't ever mention that name to me again."

"John?"

"Clark Gable." She hugged herself tighter. "Oh, the walls of Jericho are going to come tumbling down all right. And my dear husband isn't going to know what hit him. But we've got to move fast. Can you stay for a couple of hours and type up a final draft of the proposal for me?"

"Sure. My folks aren't expecting me until dinner."

"Thanks. Maybe, just maybe, this Christmas won't be a complete bust, anyway." There was a little catch in her voice.

Jane was giving her boss a comforting pat as John swept back into the room, sweaty and out of breath.

"They took off. Akiko went with them. And David," he announced. "When they come back you'll have proof that she isn't pregnant."

Casey gave Jane a surreptitious warning not to give anything away. Then she walked over to John. "Maybe I overreacted."

John looked at her skeptically.

She smiled sheepishly. "I never realized I was the jealous type. I made such a dumb scene. I'd better go down and apologize to Toho. He did stay home?"

John nodded. "Casey, I'd like to explain everything."

She touched his cheek lightly and smiled. Of all the improvisational acting she'd had to do this week, that brief little gesture decidedly took the most out of her. Even now, with all the rage and bitterness at his betrayal, she felt absolutely wretched. "Later, darling. We'll talk later," she managed to say as her head started to spin. *Oh, we'll talk later, all right, John Gallagher. We'll have ourselves one hell of a rousing talk. Believe me, I've got plenty I want to say to you.*

"No, Casey. No, I think . . ."

"I should go downstairs and attend to Toho. Whatever must he think of me?"

Casey took hold of Jane's arm and hurried her out of the room and down the stairs, quickly depositing her in the den, where she could update the Matoki file on the computer. After Casey heard the lock turn on the den door she proceeded to the living room where Toho Matoki was reading a *Newsweek* magazine.

He looked up as Casey entered, a questioning expression on his face. "Are you all right, Casey?"

"Never better," she said brightly.

"Really," Toho murmured. "An extraordinary turn of events."

Casey sat down opposite him. "I'm sorry for the scene I caused, breaking the glass and running out of the room the way I did."

Toho merely smiled. "You must love him very much, Casey."

"I certainly love her." John said emphatically as he stepped into the room. He walked over and sat down beside Casey on the sofa, putting an affectionate arm around her. "I'd marry her again, every time."

Casey could barely return a civil look. *Does he know?* she wondered. *Does he know that I know?*

"By the way, darling? Who's locked in the den?" John asked, idly stroking her arm with a feathery sweep of his fingertips.

Casey tried to ignore the traitorous little erotic currents coursing through her arm. "It's Jane." She leveled her gaze on John. "She's putting together the final proposal for the hotel project."

"I see."

John's expression was unreadable. Casey turned her attention to Toho. "I was hoping we might celebrate Christmas tomorrow with a done deal. After all, we've gone over the proposal quite thoroughly. I know the Hammond group is eager to get started. You've seemed so impressed by what I've presented. Oh, and by John's input, as well." She shot a phony smile at John. "You've been such a marvelous help through all this, darling."

Casey returned her gaze to Toho. Unfortunately, his expression was also unreadable. But, then, what else was new?

"What do you say, Toho?" She knew she was pressuring him, and Toho Matoki was not a man who liked to be pressured. But Casey was desperate. If she let him go without a signed deal, she risked losing it altogether. She was sure now that John was merely making points for himself with Matoki. He was no doubt keeping his very best ideas for later, for when he and Brenda could put together the Kirkland proposal. Sure, she thought, livid at the prospect, he'd also incorporate the Hammond proposal into his own concepts for the project and knock the socks off Toho.

Toho set down his magazine and slowly rose. He bestowed thoughtful looks on both Casey and John, but said nothing.

Casey got to her feet. "Will you at least read it over and make your decision after that? Jane will have it ready in a couple of hours."

"You don't want to rush Toho," John cautioned.

Casey felt a rush of fury. She would have liked nothing better than to confront John right there on the spot, expose him for the disreputable, underhanded bastard he really was. But that wouldn't aid her cause any, to say the least, since she'd be disastrously exposed, as well. Casey fought back her rage. She was down to the wire, and she was not going to blow it now. She smiled lovingly at John. "I'm not rushing Toho, darling. I just thought, since Jane is here assembling the proposal, why wait?"

"Let's just say it's Japanese business etiquette not to turn the screws."

"I'm not turning any screws," she said tightly.

Toho's dark eyes observed them both. "You are a most intriguing couple. I am grateful to you both." As he finished his obtuse remark, the solemn set of his lips suddenly metamorphosed into a wide smile. "And, yes. I look forward to a very festive Christmas morning." With a little bow Toho Matoki made his exit.

"Men," Casey thought despairingly. "East, West, I'll never figure either one of them out."

12

Two turtle doves . . .

JOHN STOOD INSIDE Casey's bedroom door, wearing the little crooked smile he'd stolen from Clark Gable.

"What's that all about?" he drawled, pointing to the huge blanket strung across the alcove.

"That, darling, is the wall of Jericho. And behind that wall is your bed."

"I see."

"Yes, I thought you would," Casey said wryly, "after your little chat with Brenda after Jane left this afternoon." Casey could barely control her fury. And what really made her boil was the nonchalant way John had taken the news that his little ruse was up. If anything, his spirits seemed lifted. For him, the exposure appeared to be nothing more than a relief. For the rest of the day and evening he'd even managed to play hubby with added exuberance and élan. Furthermore, he seemed to be taking a perverse pleasure in making Casey steam.

John cleared his throat, but he said nothing. Nor did he move from his post.

"I'd like to go to bed," Casey said stiffly.

John shrugged. "As a kid I never could sleep on the night before Christmas. Sure you don't want to stay up and listen for the pitter-patter of Santa and his reindeer on your roof?"

"I don't believe in Santa Claus."

"Oh? Gee, the other morning, on the couch next door, you seemed . . ."

"I was drunk. My head was spinning."

"So was mine, Casey. Mine's been spinning all week."

"The game's up, John." She could hear the catch in her throat.

"Casey," John said softly, "the game was up almost before it began." He started toward her.

Casey's hand shot up. "Don't come near me. I mean it. I thought you were my knight in shining armor. I thought you were the most wonderful . . . You're nothing but a fraud. You lied to me. You deceived me. You . . . you made a fool of me. And I . . . I asked for it. I certainly did ask for it." She shook her head. "How could I have been so naive? How could I have been so blind?"

"They say love is blind, darling."

"Don't ever call me 'darling' again. You've made a mockery of love. I don't love you, John. I never loved you. I loved this man I believed was honest, sincere, trustworthy . . ."

"Okay, Casey, I'm not a Boy Scout. If that's really what you wanted, you have been duped. But let's remember, darling, you're no Girl Scout. You play a pretty good game yourself."

Stung by his words, she felt the blood surge in her head. "Not with you, John. I wasn't playing games with you."

"And I told you, Casey, that I stopped playing games with you the minute I realized I was falling in love with you." Despite her protest, he sat down beside her on the bed. "I think it happened under the mistletoe that first night."

"Stop it. Do you really think I'd believe a word you said now?" She looked straight into his eyes, her expression defiant.

"No, I don't suppose you would, darling."

She flinched at his continued use of "darling," but she said nothing, knowing he was doing it to get a rise out of her.

He stood up, but he made no move away from the bed. "I could have given you away to Matoki, you know. Anytime. Exposed your game. Ruined the deal for you."

"Not without ruining it for yourself. Did you think I'd never find out who you really were? Who Brenda was? Did you think if the Kirkland group waltzed off with the deal I'd put my time . . . my heart . . . my soul into, I wouldn't dig until I found out who was responsible for stealing the project out from under me? And did you think, once I'd learned you were sitting pretty in some lavish office in the Kirkland Building, that I'd keep my mouth shut out of some perverse concept of loyalty to the man who destroyed me? Not on your life, Gallagher. I would have been on the phone to Matoki faster than you could toss off a jingle bells."

John merely smiled at her vituperative attack. "Well, darling, now I know where you got your outstanding reputation in the business. So this is the real Casey Croyden. Hard as nails. Vindictive. Indomitable."

"All of that," she answered hotly.

His smile broadened. "Beautiful, wanton and tough. I like that combination, darling."

"It's not going to work this time, John. It's over. Truly over." She rose and strode across the room to the make-shift curtain, pulling it aside. "Please go to bed."

He approached her, took hold of her hand clenching the blanket. "I never dreamed any of this would happen, Casey."

Her eyes shot up to his, and she tried desperately to ignore his touch. Even now she felt he was capable of manipulating her heart. Her poor woebegone, battered heart. "No, I bet you never dreamed I'd take you right into my home, serve Matoki up to you on a silver platter. You were lucky all right, John. You hit pay dirt with Matoki. And got me as a bonus to boot." She closed her eyes. "A temporary bonus, anyway." She swayed a little.

John went to support her, but she shoved him away, in the process, tugging at the blanket that was still clutched in her fist. The walls of Jericho came tumbling down along with the heavy metal curtain rod that had held the blanket in place. Par for the course, the walls tumbled down right on top of Casey. She let out a sharp cry of pain as the bar struck her head before crashing to the floor. The blanket fell over her like a shroud.

John started to lift the cover off of her, but Casey screamed, "Don't touch me. Don't you ever touch me again, you bastard." She was kicking her way out of the blanket as they heard a knock on the door.

"Casey, are you all right?"

Akiko. Casey sighed. That woman's timing was impeccable.

Casey's head popped out of the blanket. "Yes . . . I'm fine."

John was scowling. "No, you're not," he said sharply. "Akiko, Casey cut herself. Could you run and get some antiseptic cream and bandages?"

"Liar," Casey said after Akiko had left. "You just like humiliating me in front of the Matokis. That's been your game all along. Make me look a fool so Matoki would never buy my proposal."

John, up to now in top form, lost some of his control. "You've done a good enough job of that on your own. I'm the one who repeatedly saved your neck, remember? And I happen to still be crazy about that neck of yours."

Casey felt something warm and wet on her cheek as she glared at him. Thinking it an unbidden tear, she swiped at it, only to discover it wasn't a teardrop but blood.

"I'm bleeding," she said, shocked.

"See, I'm not the liar you think I am," he drawled.

Casey looked utterly forlorn as she sank to the floor, the blanket wrapped around her. She closed her eyes. All her energy was gone. All her hopes, her dreams, her fantasies . . . gone.

"Does it hurt that much?" John asked softly, joining her on the floor, gently brushing a wayward strand of hair from her cut forehead.

Casey's eyelids fluttered open, her big blue eyes lifting to his face. "Yes, yes, it hurts that much," she said in a bare whisper.

"Poor darling," John said, reaching out for the box of tissues on a nearby nightstand. He pulled one out to dab away the blood. "It's not too bad. A surface wound. It won't even leave a scar."

Casey grabbed the tissue away and blew her nose. "Oh, yes it will. It'll leave a scar all right."

"Casey. . ." His eyes roved her face. "I intended to explain."

"When? After you clinched the deal with Matoki for yourself? Well, not if I can do anything about it. Toho's probably reading my finished proposal right this minute. And let me tell you, it's going to knock him off his feet. Before he leaves, I'm going to do everything in my power to get his name on the dotted line." She hesitated. "Unless you play even dirtier than I think. I suppose you could blow it for me by telling Matoki the truth."

"I thought you said I wouldn't do that. That it would blow the deal for me as well."

"That's true. Until he signs, you'll think you still have a fighting chance."

He stared at her in silence for several moments, his expression intense. "I never give up without a fight. Not when it's something I really want." He leaned and touched his lips softly to hers just as Akiko came rushing into the room with a makeshift first-aid kit. Right behind her was Toho and the rest of the "reindeer." Casey, who'd been about to shove John away, had no recourse but to go on playing the game she herself had started.

"Poor John, he's frantic with worry over a little scratch." Casey smiled at the anxious faces of her house guests as Akiko bent to have a look. Casey's eyes met Akiko's. "But, then, you know how husbands are, Akiko. Loving husbands, anyway."

Akiko delicately cleaned away the wound with a wet washcloth. "It is not a deep cut, Casey. You will be fine."

"That's what I told her," John piped in.

Wes came over to be a closer look at the damage. As he bent down, he gave John a searing glance, then studied Casey with nothing short of abject pity. "How'd it happen?"

Casey took a breath. So Wes knew, too. She glanced across the room at Brenda, who stood in the doorway, looking profoundly miserable. Wes looked quite awful himself. Poor Wes. He really did love Brenda. Well, at least Brenda had had the guts to finally admit the truth to him herself.

Casey put a hand out to Wes. "It was a dumb accident, Wes. I'll be fine."

Wes didn't look convinced.

Toho stepped over to observe Akiko's ministrations to the wound. After thoroughly drying the area, she carefully applied antiseptic cream and then a bandage.

"Most unfortunate, Casey," Toho said regretfully. "You do seem rather accident-prone since our arrival here in Vermont. I truly hope we have not brought you bad luck."

"Oh, no, you didn't bring bad luck, Toho," David said, trying to help out. "Casey's been accident-prone since we were kids. Remember that time—"

"Oh, shut up, David," Casey snapped, then immediately gasped. "I'm sorry. I didn't mean . . ."

David grinned. "It's okay, Sis. You've told me to shut up once or twice in our lives. I just didn't want Toho here to think he was in any way responsible."

Tears welled in Casey's eyes as she looked up at David. "No, I know. I know you were only trying to help." Her gaze shifted to Wes. "I'm really very grateful. Really. . . I am." The tears were rolling down her cheek. She knew in another minute she'd be bawling, but she didn't seem to be able to do anything about it.

John slipped his arms under Casey and lifted her up. "She'll be fine. The trauma and all. She just needs a good night's sleep. Right, darling?"

Casey couldn't respond. Held close in John's strong arms, she was filled with such an odd combination of emotions. She felt his eyes burning into her, and she tried to avoid them. Not raising her own eyes, she finally managed a weak, "I am tired."

It was Akiko who firmly shooed everyone out. At the door, just before she closed it, Akiko smiled brightly at

John and Casey. "Tomorrow, all will be well. Christmas morning. Ah, how exciting it will be. A true New England Christmas morning."

She closed the door quietly, and Casey, still in John's arms, listened silently to Akiko's light footsteps fading down the hall.

Slowly she turned to meet John's gaze. "What do you think she meant? Tomorrow, all will be well? Do you think . . . ?" Casey absently ran her tongue over her dry lips. "Do you think you could put me down, John?"

"I don't want to."

"Please," she said nervously. "I want you to."

John made no move to release her. Nor did he respond in any way.

The silence hummed, momentarily enveloping Casey.

Without moving a muscle, John finally said, "You know what I want, Casey."

Her heart slammed against the walls of her chest. She wasn't sure that if he did put her down, she could remain standing on her own two feet. Maybe he realized the problem. In three long strides, he carried her to her bed and gently lowered her on it.

What Casey hadn't bargained on was John stretching out beside her. She started to protest, but found herself looking into his dark eyes, seeing the tenderness, even a hint of pain, reflected in them. She was unaware of the tortured expression on her own face.

"Oh, John. You really did knock me off my feet." Even now, hating him as she told herself she did, she still found herself wanting him. No, "want" was too weak a word. Craving him. Yes, craving him. What a fool. What an absolute fool she was.

Without taking his eyes off her, his mouth moved over hers. Even as she swore she would not respond, Casey felt her lips part, her tongue boldly slip between his lips, seeking his tongue, kissing him back greedily. Her stomach fluttered, her heart pounded, her mind ignored the string of warnings trying in vain to be heard over the raucous beat of her heart. And John's. *Two hearts . . . beating as one.*

It was John who pulled away first. When he did, Casey shivered, a tremor that shook her whole body. He touched her hair, lightly kissed her bandaged wound, then rose from her bed and said a tender good-night.

When he got to the archway of the alcove he turned back to her. "Shall I resurrect the walls of Jericho?"

Casey pulled herself together. She realized that a makeshift wall would never be effective enough. What she needed to do, and do quickly, was to resurrect a more permanent, impenetrable wall around her shattered heart. In answer to John's question she merely said in a flat, even tone, "No, that won't be necessary."

THE GROUP THAT GATHERED round the tree on Christmas morning looked about as cheerful as mourners at a wake. Except for Toho and Akiko. They were positively brimming with good cheer. Casey suggested they open their gifts first, and they did so with eager abandon, seemingly oblivious to the forced smiles and strangled oohs and ahs of the rest of the group as they opened and displayed each of their presents. Akiko and Toho were delighted with their New England gifts—a tin shaped like a log cabin, filled with grade A maple syrup, from David; a Vermont sweatshirt with a cow motif from Wes, locally crafted pottery chimes from Brenda; and a framed photograph, circa 1780, of Dorset's Main Street from John. The Matokis gasped in sheer delight as they opened their last gift, this one from Casey.

"How beautiful," Akiko murmured as she delicately lifted the miniature pair of jeweled angels with gossamer wings from their box. They were a bedazzling Christmas tree ornament. Akiko read aloud the little card attached to the gift, which explained that the angels had been designed and made by a famous Vermont artisan, Lyla Paulie, a woman now in her late eighties.

"She's sort of the Grandma Moses of New England crafts," Casey said.

A tender smile lit Akiko's face. "We shall display our angels every Christmas and think so happily of our wonderful Christmas holiday with all of you."

Toho nodded in agreement. He seemed deeply touched by everyone's thoughtfulness. "Now you must all open your gifts," Toho said.

With forced enthusiasm, they all set about the task of opening their gifts. Soon the living room floor was laden with jewelry boxes, ties, perfume, silver earrings and the like.

Brenda postponed opening her gift from Wes until she'd unwrapped all the rest. She looked over at him, smiled hesitantly and blinked several times as she slowly, meticulously unwrapped the silver paper and red ribbon. Casey and John, both of whom still had their gifts from each other to open, sat quietly and watched Brenda.

Inside the wrapping was a thin oblong box. Brenda started to open it, then stopped, laying her palm flat on the lid. "Maybe I'll wait...till later," she said nervously, her gaze shooting back to Wes.

"No," he said softly, "open it now. I hope you'll like it. It's...not exchangeable."

Before she lifted the lid, she turned to Casey, locking eyes with her. "I just want you to know, Casey..." She stopped, her eyes watering. Then she started over again. "I just want you to know . . . I really am your friend. Maybe there've been times you doubted it—you had reason. But I hope I . . . never give you cause to doubt my friendship for you again."

It took a moment for Casey to realize the full impact of Brenda's words. When she did, tears welled up in her eyes, as well. Akiko dug tissues out of the wide pocket of her kimono and handed one to each woman, using one herself to delicately dab at her eyes.

Still teary-eyed, Brenda opened Wes's gift. It was an airline ticket to Paris, Wes's next assignment.

"We won't return until mid-January," Wes said, his eyes fixed on Brenda. "Are you sure you can get extra time off?"

Brenda shook her head. "I'm sure I can't."

"Oh," Wes murmured.

Brenda smiled at Wes, then shifted her gaze to John and Casey. "But it won't be necessary. I mailed in my resignation yesterday afternoon." Her eyes glistened as she looked back at Wes. "So I'm unemployed as of now. We can stay in Paris as long as you like."

Wes reached out for her hand, held it tightly in his. "Maybe after Paris we can tour the Costa del Sol or something. And after that . . . well anything's possible."

A becoming rosy hue graced Brenda's cheeks. "Yes," she whispered, "anything's possible."

There were a few moments of silence, and then Toho nodded in Casey and John's direction. "You must open your gifts from each other now."

John glanced at Casey before he undid the wrapping of the gift box. Inside was a gold-leaf and leather-bound first edition of Robert Frost's poems. John lifted the exquisite book from the box, carefully opening to the first page, where Casey had written an inscription. She hoped in vain that he would read it to himself.

"'To my dearest husband. There shall never be another Christmas quite like this. All my love for helping me to believe miracles really can happen. Your adoring wife, Casey.'" After John finished reading the inscription aloud, he leaned over and kissed Casey tenderly. "Thank you, darling." His eyes sparkled. You'll have to read a sonnet to me each night before we go to bed."

It was all Casey could do to keep from saying "Over my dead body." She'd almost retrieved the book from under the tree yesterday with the intention of ripping out the inscribed page. But she couldn't bring herself to destroy a magnificent first edition that had cost her a small fortune. Besides, she was more determined than ever to carry the ruse to its bitter end in the hope that Matoki would come through with an okay on the Hammond deal before he and Akiko left for Tokyo tomorrow. So far, he hadn't said a single word about the proposal.

"Open yours now, darling," John coaxed.

Casey stared down at the gold-wrapped box in her lap. She told herself that the only gift she'd be pleased to see was a photocopy of a letter signed by John similar to the one Brenda had mailed Kirkland. If he had any scruples at all . . .

Inside the large box was a tiny red satin box hidden in the midst of a sea of red polka dot tissue paper. Casey compressed her lips as she lifted the lid, an involuntary gasp escaping her.

John leaned over and took the gold-and-ruby wedding band from the box. Before Casey knew what was happening, he was removing the plain gold band from her finger, replacing it with the new, shimmering eighteen-karat gold and ruby band. "I can't tell you how long I've wanted to give you this, darling." Her jaw clenched as he swept her in his arms and kissed her. When he released her, John grinned at Toho and Akiko. "We were in such a hurry to get married, I didn't have time to pick out a proper ring for Casey." He nuzzled her neck. "She swept me right off my feet and I've been floating ever since."

Akiko looked admiringly at the ring. "It is very beautiful, John. A perfect gift."

"Yes," Toho agreed, sharing a little smile with his wife, "a perfect gift."

David murmured, "Great-looking ring, Sis."

Brenda gave Casey a warm hug. And Wes gave Casey a sympathetic pat on the back.

Then all three gathered up their gifts and went off together into the kitchen to get breakfast started.

Casey was about to join them, when Akiko gave Toho a gentle nudge and a coquettish smile. "And now for your gift to Casey and John, honorable husband."

Casey, still taken aback by the wedding ring John had given her, stared at the Matokis with a dazed expression. "But you already gave us our gift. The lovely Japanese tea set. . . ."

Toho rose and gave a little bow. Then he retrieved the neatly clipped sheaf of papers from the deep pocket of his lounging kimono.

Casey held her breath.

"I am most impressed by your proposal, Casey." Toho looked at John. "And equally impressed by your input, John." He slowly rolled the proposal up in his hand. "I must, however, tell you that I have decided not to accept the Hammond deal."

Casey couldn't believe her ears. "But . . ."

Toho waved a silencing hand. "The two of you have made me realize that the Hammond Corporation is not the appropriate partner I seek."

"Wait a second, Toho," John broke in." In all fairness to Casey—"

"No, please, John. Hear me out," Toho said, cutting him off.

"You can't have gotten a better proposal. Unless . . ." Casey shot John a hard, accusatory look.

"Please, Casey," Akiko said softly, "you mustn't be upset." Akiko gave Toho a cheerful smile. "Do not be so long-winded, my dear husband."

Toho gave a little chuckle. "Yes, yes. It is only my poor attempt at drama."

Casey and John both gave Toho puzzled looks.

"You see, I would like to make a counterproposal," Toho went on.

"A counterproposal?" Casey echoed.

"Yes," he said solemnly. "In coming to New England, I have found the perfect team to head my new American-Japanese hotel development. A husband-wife team. You, Casey and you, John. I am offering you a position of importance and prominence with the honorable Matoki Corporation in Tokyo. This project would hopefully be the start of many you would head, both in Japan and the United States and ultimately throughout Asia and Europe. I have great plans. And the two of you are perfectly suited to lead the new enterprise."

John and Casey shared astonished looks. It was John who spoke. "You mean you want both of us—as a team—to head this project and other projects in the future?"

"Oh, yes, it must be both of you. You work brilliantly together."

"And we are greatly impressed by your commitment to each other," Akiko added. "Very rarely do we see a couple who so instinctively respond to each other's needs. We are touched by the tenderness you show each other. Even your squabbles flow out of love. We know," Akiko said with sparkling eyes. "It is much the same for Toho and I."

"Of course," Toho added, "it goes without saying that you would both receive vice-presidential appointments in my company. But titles are the least of it. We are a growing company with great prospects for the future. For your future, as well, I hope."

Casey was flabbergasted. She was being handed the job offer of a lifetime. Of a thousand lifetimes.

With one horrible catch. It was a package deal with the devil. A marital package deal from hell. It was untenable, impossible, unthinkable...

"Think it over. You need not give an immediate answer," Toho said. "Talk to each other. Weigh the pros and the cons, as you say."

Casey swallowed hard. There was nothing to think about. Toho was offering the job to a happily married couple. She and John weren't happily anything, least of all married. Once Christmas was over, Casey planned never to set eyes on the unscrupulous John Gallagher ever again. And he could take his jeweled ring with him. Swept off his feet, indeed.

"Ah, can you hear? Carolers," Akiko exclaimed. "Let's go listen."

In the silence, they could hear the group of singers approaching Casey's porch. Toho took Akiko's hand. "Yes. Meanwhile, perhaps you and John can consider my offer."

Toho and Akiko were halfway across the room, when Casey called out, "Wait. There's no need for John and I to talk it over. We already have . . . our answer."

Then, before Casey could turn down Toho's dream offer John spoke up. "Casey's right, Toho. We do have our answer. And that answer is yes. We'd have to be fools to turn down the offer of a lifetime. And we're not fools, are we, darling?"

Toho's eyes gleamed. "No, I never for a moment took either of you for fools. I am very pleased."

"Yes," Akiko said brightly, "we are both so pleased. Now we shall become true and lasting friends."

Casey was speechless. Her head was spinning. Was John crazy? Did he actually think she'd be willing to keep up this insane ruse indefinitely? Even for the job offer of a lifetime? She followed Akiko and Toho into the hall.

"No, wait," Casey cried out.

13

We wish you a Merry Christmas . . .

JOHN CAUGHT HOLD of Casey's arm as she got to the arched entryway. He pulled her to him and gave her a mischievous smile. "Look up, darling. Mistletoe." Before she could utter another word, his mouth descended for a torrid, breath-stealing kiss.

She gasped as he released her mouth. "John, are you crazy?"

"Yes," he murmured. "I'm crazy about you."

"I can't take that job. I can't go on indefinitely pretending we're married."

He drew her a few inches away, keeping a firm hold of her shoulders. "Shh. Keep your voice down." He pointed to the group gathered at the open front door. Wes, Brenda and David had joined the Matokis to listen to the carolers' festive renditions of some Christmas classics.

John was smiling his impossible Gable smile. "We'll pull it off, darling. After all, we are a terrific team."

"Oh, John, what have you done?" Casey moaned as he led her down the hall to join the others. He grabbed their coats from the coat tree by the door and they slipped them on.

Toho and Akiko made space for them at the open door. "Such a lovely tradition," Akiko said softly to Casey.

"Yes, a lovely New England traditional Christmas," Toho agreed, sharing a curiously sly smile with his wife before gazing at John and Casey with a most inscrutable expression. "And there is yet one more tradition we might speak of on this auspicious occasion, the time-honored tradition of marriage."

Casey swallowed hard. She could not look Toho in the eye as she murmured, "Yes, that tradition." *Okay, Casey, here's your chance to come clean. This is it. Now or never. Forget about saving face. Time to save your neck...*

"As you know, Casey, John," Toho went on solemnly, "Akiko and I have been blissfully married for twenty-eight years."

David, trying to break the tension, began applauding. "Terrific. Great. Congratulations. That's quite a record, especially these days."

Toho raised a brow and Brenda poked David in the ribs.

"As I was saying..." Toho paused, as if he'd lost track of his thoughts.

John took Casey's hand and gave it a little squeeze.

"You were speaking of the time-honored tradition of marriage, honorable husband," Akiko said with a teasing smile.

Toho gave her a rueful look. "Ah, yes. The venerable tradition of marriage."

Casey opened her mouth to speak. She couldn't bear it any longer. She had to tell the Matokis the truth. She and John were making a mockery of marriage. How could she stand there and pretend...

"So, it is my fondest hope, as it is Akiko's—" Toho again paused, giving John and Casey piercing looks

"—should you two decide to actually become married, that Akiko and I will be invited to your wedding."

A ripple of giggles escaped Akiko's lips. "Oh, yes, Toho and I would love to see a traditional New England wedding. And knowing the two of you and your most creative friends, it would also be full of exciting surprises."

Toho chuckled as he observed the astonished expressions of the group. He gave his wife and cohort a self-satisfied wink.

Each of the listeners received Matoki's revelations with truly stunned disbelief.

"You knew we weren't married?" John muttered, his tone incredulous.

Casey had to grab on to the doorknob for support. "Since . . . when?"

"Oh, the whole time," Akiko said brightly.

"The whole time?" David exclaimed in amazement.

Toho gave a little bow. "Soon after we accepted your invitation, one of my staff learned that you and Wes Carpenter had been divorced, Casey," he said in a matter-of-fact voice, giving Wes a nod of acknowledgment. "Naturally we assumed Casey would explain when we arrived."

Casey responded defensively. "But . . . but you even brought the matching *yukata*s—one for John . . ."

"Oh, yes. I bought those right after we accepted the invitation. Just before . . ."

Casey nodded. Akiko didn't need to finish.

"Wait a second," John broke in. "You went along . . . No, no, you more than went along with our game. You . . ."

Toho chuckled. "You, John, have much to learn of the playful side of the Japanese character. It is inconceivable to you that Akiko and I could...how shall I say, play a few pranks of our own?"

John laughed dryly. "I suppose I didn't spend enough time in Japan, after all."

Akiko clapped her hands mirthfully. "From the moment we arrived, you engaged in a delightfully amusing...shall I say...improvisation? It was only fair that Toho and I join in on the fun." Another spurt of giggles erupted from her lips.

"Delightful?" Casey stared numbly at Toho, who was smiling broadly and exchanging affectionate glances with Akiko.

"Amusing?" John muttered, still astounded at the amazing turn of events.

"Yes, delightful and thoroughly amusing. Akiko and I never dreamed this holiday would turn out to be so unique," Toho said amiably. "All of you performed your roles admirably. But, of course, Casey, you and John deserve the most credit. Both of you were remarkably quick thinking, inventive, creative, quite ingenious at every opportunity."

"And you, Toho, our master prankster *extraordinaire*, deserve the last laugh," Casey said with grudging respect. "A laugh that you must have gotten when we agreed to take you up on your job offer. I should have realized it was too good to be true. Well, I take my hat off to you both. Talk about award-winning performances." She looked over at the only "professional" actor among them. "What would Stanislavski say, brother David?"

David gave a rueful laugh. "You know what he'd say? He'd say—" the actor hunched over to suggest old age and affected an exaggerated Russian accent —"Vell, David, perhaps you should haf studied in Japan all these years instead of vasting your time at the Actors' Studio."

Casey slowly surveyed the entire group, a blossoming smile animating her features. When her eyes met Toho Matoki's, she shook her head and broke into laughter. Shortly she was laughing so hard she had to hold on to John for support. John hugged Casey tightly and started laughing, too. And then the others joined in, drowning out the earnest carolers who were still serenading them. The carolers seemed delighted with the laughter and began singing another round of Christmas standards for the cheerful group.

John met Casey's eyes. "For what its worth, darling, I still plan to make an honest woman of you. I've adored being your husband. I promise to play the pants off of the part if you'll give me the role permanently. I love you, Casey." He gave her his irresistible Gable grin.

Casey's blue eyes shimmered. "Oh, John...I love you, too," Whatever else happened, Casey knew she'd gotten what she most wanted this Christmas—and for all Christmases to come.

Toho interrupted the touching embrace. "Please, John, Casey, there yet remains one more misunderstanding I must clear up."

All eyes fixed on Toho.

He smiled warmly at Casey and John. "I do not have need of a last laugh. Akiko and I have had a most generous share of laughter throughout this wonderful holiday week." Toho's eyes twinkled. "What I genuinely need now is the two of you. My offer was most sincere. Your actions this past week were wonderful examples of American ingenuity at its best. At this juncture, the Matoki Corporation can benefit greatly from this clever problem solving. I could not ask for a more perfect team to lead my new venture."

Casey was speechless. For once that week, so was John.

"I think he means it," David piped up.

Brenda and Wes nodded agreement.

Akiko took gentle hold of Casey's hand. "And we do so hope you truly mean to invite us to your wedding."

"Yes. Oh, yes," Casey murmured, her glistening blue eyes sweeping the group and coming to rest finally on John. "Everyone's invited, right, darling? My best childhood girlfriend, her adoring boyfriend, my fiercely loyal brother, my shrewd new boss and his equally gifted wife . . . and especially . . . most especially . . . my darling husband."

Casey and John kissed lovingly as the holiday guests smiled on them. The carolers on the front porch sang, "'We wish you a merry Christmas . . .'"

And, indeed, a very merry Christmas was had by all.

COMING NEXT MONTH

A compelling novel of deadly revenge and passion
from Harlequin's bestselling international
romance author Penny Jordan

POWER PLAY

Eleven years had passed but the
terror of that night was something
Pepper Minesse would never
forget. Fueled by revenge against
the four men who had brutally
shattered her past, she set in
motion a deadly plan to destroy
their futures.

Available in February!

 Harlequin Books ®

HPP-1A

You'll flip . . . your pages won't!
Read paperbacks *hands-free* with

Book Mate · I

The perfect "mate" for all your romance paperbacks

**Traveling • Vacationing • At Work • In Bed • Studying
• Cooking • Eating**

Perfect size for all standard paperbacks, this wonderful invention makes reading a pure pleasure! Ingenious design holds paperback books OPEN and FLAT so even wind can't ruffle pages — leaves your hands free to do other things. Reinforced, wipe-clean vinyl-covered holder flexes to let you turn pages without undoing the strap . . . supports paperbacks so well, they have the strength of hardcovers!

Pages turn WITHOUT opening the strap.

SEE-THROUGH STRAP

Reinforced back stays flat.

Built in bookmark

BOOK MARK

BACK COVER HOLDING STRIP

10˝ x 7¼˝ opened.
Snaps closed for easy carrying, too.

Harlequin Superromance®

LET THE GOOD TIMES ROLL...

Add some Cajun spice to liven up your New Year's celebrations and join Superromance for a romantic tour of the rich Acadian marshlands and the legendary Louisiana bayous.

Starting in January 1990, we're launching CAJUN MELODIES, a three-book tribute to the fun-loving people who've enriched America by introducing us to crawfish étouffé and gumbo, zydeco music and the Saturday night party, the *fais-dodo*. And learn about loving, Cajun-style, as you meet the tall, dark, handsome men who win their ladies' hearts with a beautiful, haunting melody....

Book One: *Julianne's Song*, January 1990
Book Two: *Catherine's Song*, February 1990
Book Three: *Jessica's Song*, March 1990

The Pirate
JAYNE ANN KRENTZ

At the heart of every powerful romance story lies a legend. There are many romantic legends and countless modern variations on them, but they all have one thing in common: They are tales of brave, resourceful women who must gentle and tame the powerful, passionate men who are their true mates.

The enormous appeal of Jayne Ann Krentz lies in her ability to create modern-day versions of these classic romantic myths, and her LADIES AND LEGENDS trilogy showcases this talent. Believing that a storyteller who can bring legends to life deserves special attention, Harlequin has chosen the first book of the trilogy—THE PIRATE—to receive our Award of Excellence. Look for it in February.

AE-PIR-1